Samuel French Acting Edition

The Ring Sisters

by Charles Laurence

I0591826

‖ SAMUEL FRENCH ‖

SAMUELFRENCH.COM   **SAMUELFRENCH.CO.UK**

FOR PRODUCTION ENQUIRIES

UNITED STATES AND CANADA
Info@SamuelFrench.com
1-866-598-8449

UNITED KINGDOM AND EUROPE
Plays@SamuelFrench.co.uk
020-7255-4302

Each title is subject to availability from Samuel French, depending upon country of performance. Please be aware that *THE RING SISTERS* may not be licensed by Samuel French in your territory. Professional and amateur producers should contact the nearest Samuel French office or licensing partner to verify availability.

MUSIC USE NOTE

IMPORTANT BILLING AND CREDIT REQUIREMENTS

CAST
(In Order of Appearance)

DOLORES PAYNE
FRED PAYNE
SAM JOHNSON
SILVA RING
BO BERGMAN
NICKY DONATELLO
LOLA WALES

The Riverside Penthouse of Silva Ring in London:

Act I

Scene 1:   Mid-afternoon in June
Scene 2:   The following afternoon
Scene 3:   Evening

Act II

Scene 1:   Late that night
Scene 2:   Late Saturday afternoon
Scene 3:   A month later

THE CAST

<u>DOLORES PAYNE.</u> Middle-aged housekeeper/dresser to Silva. Very forthright. Eccentric, caustic, rude. Plays at being 'a character', wears items of Silva's wardrobe to bizarre effect.

<u>FRED PAYNE.</u> 40's, pale, lean, wiry build. Brother of Dolores. A petty criminal, harmless. Nervous and easily bullied. Usually looks unhappy.

<u>SAM JOHNSON.</u> 50's. A tough, successful agent. A smart, conventional dresser. Charming and soothing manner. Avuncular with eye on the main chance.

<u>SILVA RING/IRIS</u>. 53 but looks 40. A charismatic, singing superstar. Great energy, determination. Lives on adrenaline, manipulative. Transformed into IRIS she is steely, cruel and slightly sinister.

<u>BO BERGMAN.</u> Late thirties. Large, big boned Swede. Blond, academic/explorer. Earnest, humorless, correct, single minded. Swedish/American accent.

<u>NICKY DONATELLO.</u> Thirty. Macho, professional footballer. A go-getter. Sexy, good physique. Sunny, jolly charm. Life's a laugh.

<u>LOLA WALES.</u> Seventies. Short, with a drink problem, she staggers happily through life. Feisty, sharp and bright, she's nobody's fool.

ACT I

Scene 1

(The Docklands flat of SILVA RING. Top floor of a converted warehouse.)
(Action takes place in living area.
Upstage right—an opening leading to lobby and front door.
Backstage center—large studio window overlooking river and iron fire escape.
Backstage left—door to SILVA's bedroom.
Downstage left—opening to kitchen, loo and staff quarters.
Stage right—books, record and hi-fi units, telephone and answering machine.
Stage left—drinks unit.
Center stage—seating units around coffee table.
Backstage—on rostrum, small table with drawers and chair by window.)
(Furnishings are modern, expensive, chrome and lacquer but comfortable. Female singer belting out a number on record player as curtain rises.)
(DOLORES, mid-fifties, is sitting in chair with feet on coffee table, smoking and drinking from a beer can. She wears a filmy, flamboyant, multi-colored wrap and tatty, fluffy bedroom slippers. She is reading the Financial Times. Telephone rings, she turns off record with remote control, groans and ambles over to pick up phone.)

DOLORES. What now? ... No dear, Sam's not here. Should he be? ... Nobody tells me anything ... Me? Dreadful. It's the feet again, all those years in the Ballet Rambert. *(Doorbell rings.)* Hang on, that might be him now. *(She exits to front door and re-enters quickly.)* Get in, wipe your boots and keep quiet. *(FRED follows her in as she picks up phone. He is lean and nervous, younger than his sister DOLORES. He glances quickly at the room and hugs close to the wall.)* False alarm, dear, only my jailbird brother ... Yes, Famous Fred the Forger, only man to flood the market with counterfeit rupees. Gloria wants to know if you're going straight?

FRED. What!

DOLORES. That's frightened him, been in and out like a randy rabbit all his life. Makes me sick when I think of the money I wasted putting him through art school ... What d'you mean, so it's all my fault? I expected him to paint green ladies not banknotes ... I won't, bye. *(Hangs up.)* Cheeky hussy's getting sophisticated. Sit down a minute.

(DOLORES gets envelope from record shelf.)

FRED. Can't we have a cup of tea in the kitchen?

DOLORES. This isn't a social call. If you want refreshment, I daresay there's some dregs in the can.

FRED. I ain't accustomed to all this space. Makes me jumpy.

DOLORES. Well, stop staring at the walls. Keep your eyes on the floor and pretend it's a cell.

FRED. Only the Governor's office had a carpet.

DOLORES. Give me strength. Would you relax if I rattled a tin mug up and down the fire escape?

FRED. Don't mock. It ain't easy outside.

DOLORES. Don't tell me, I've had to spend my whole life outside. Have you got Silva's new passport?

FRED. Yes.

(FRED fishes out a passport and exchanges it for the envelope DOLORES holds out.)

DOLORES. It's a good neat job. *(DOLORES sits and opens passport.)* Born 1960!! She's out of her mind. My guess would be she fought in the war.

FRED. That's what she told me to put.

DOLORES. 1960 indeed. The customs will laugh in her face and submit her to anal searches.

FRED. Dolores, this envelope's been tampered with and there's money missing.

DOLORES. I took my commission.

FRED. What for?

DOLORES. For your own good. It's in the Building Society ready for your next bail.

FRED. I might stay out of trouble this time.

DOLORES. Fred, you're a grown man, love. It's your pattern, you always get caught.

FRED. I do, don't I?

DOLORES. You've been too ambitious. Your Mona Lisa was a lovely bit of work but Sotheby's were bound to get suspicious.

FRED. Clever bastards!

DOLORES. Stick with me. I'll get you lots more passport work. Easy money and safer.

FRED. Not if they all turn vicious like Miss Ring. Gripped me by the throat she did, said if I ever told anyone she'd see me in a concrete overcoat by nightfall.

DOLORES. You never could take a joke.

FRED. She meant it. She's having it off with that Donatello bloke—it's the Italian connection.

DOLORES. She's also sung with Sinatra and Minelli, loves pasta and she's had audiences with assorted popes.

FRED. There you are, she's run by the Mafia.

DOLORES. Don't talk bloody daft, she's British.

FRED. I don't tangle with the mob. Tell her I'll have her driving license fixed in a couple of days.

DOLORES. She's had one for years.

FRED. Not with 1960 on.

DOLORES. Fred, was there a date of birth on the original documents she gave you?

FRED. Yes, nineteen hundred and cigarette burn.

DOLORES. That's something. I wasn't even sure it was this century. *(Doorbell rings.)* My fallen arches can't stand this treadmill. Here, if it's not a tradesman or sexual maniac, you bugger off sharpish.

(She exits. FRED gets by a wall. Voices off. Hellos, etc. DOLORES enters with SAM JOHNSON, SILVA's manager. Fifties, easy quick charm, conservative good suit. He carries a briefcase. FRED begins to sidle out along the wall.)

DOLORES. Gloria from your office called.

SAM. Oh, thanks. Is Silva back?

DOLORES. Not yet. Want a drink, Sam?

SAM. Er .. yes, why not? *(He lays his case on table by window and lays out papers and artwork. Spots tail end of FRED as he vanishes.)* Hello.

DOLORES. Won't bother to introduce you, he just left.

SAM. I'm used to it. Only a mother loves an agent.

DOLORES. *(At drinks.)* That was my brother, Fred.

SAM. Not famous Fred the Forger?

DOLORES. Yes, having a little holiday outside, he needed a break. So if you want any small artwork done like VAT invoices, airline tickets or an exclusive Elton John contract, we'd be grateful.

SAM. I run a legit business, you know that.

DOLORES. I know you got a sharp lawyer.

SAM. He's a pussycat compared to your accountant. *(DOLORES gives SAM a drink. He punches phone number.)* Hope Silva's remembered she's got an appointment.

DOLORES. There's 'copulating interview 3.30' scrawled in the diary.

SAM. Good. *(To phone.)* Gloria, did you check with Dr. Bergman? Great, he'll be on his way. Give me the calls ... scrub it ... I'll call her back ... forget it ... No, let Benjy sweat a bit ... ha, that is out of the woodwork, their last hit was '83 ... that it? Fine, I should be back in an hour. *(Hangs up and drifts back to window.)* You know, every time I come here, I'm amazed at how smashing this view of the river is?

DOLORES. Same here. My slave quarters survey a derelict warehouse and a vibrant kiddies playground.

SAM. You do alright, Dolores. There can't be many housekeepers with a Swiss bank account.

DOLORES. My regular flights to Zurich are mercy trips to visit my old dancing teacher.

SAM. Ha! You're extra colorful today.

DOLORES. Yes, another of Madam's hand me downs.

SAM. The Palladium '81. She opened the act in that.

DOLORES. Dirty cow didn't even have it cleaned before she passed it on.

SAM. Right, Uncle Sam's listening. What's really getting you down Dolores? Let the bile flow.

DOLORES. That bleeding footballer for a start.

SAM. Nicky's harmless enough.

DOLORES. He's an irritating little bastard to have underfoot. Ponces about like a chorus girl, always flashing his legs. Silva don't need that kind of publicity. She's got a great voice.

SAM. Does her good to be seen with a young stud. She is still a sex symbol.

DOLORES. Have you seen her first thing in the morning?

SAM. Don't! That's a very private moment for most of us.

(Front door slams.)

DOLORES. Red alert!

(SILVA RING explodes into the room scattering coat, tote bag and shoes on her way to flop onto the sofa units. She wears a trouser suit with silver jewelry and a wig. A fantastic wig, pale platinum blonde with strands of shining silver intertwined. Hair you could recognize from the back row of Wembley Stadium. A trademark, theatrical, astonishing. She is stylish, sexy and her age is her secret.)

SILVA. Thank god I didn't read my horoscope this morning, it must have been horrendous ... I'm out to everyone, Dolores, everyone.

(DOLORES is picking up the debris.)

SAM. Shall I vanish?
SILVA. Hello Sam. No, stay, you're like family or furniture.
SAM. Thanks, I think.
SILVA. Watch over me while I sink into a blessed coma. Dolores, what in Hades is that!?
DOLORES. I'd say a beercan—do I win a prize?
SILVA. Chuck, it, will you. It offends.

(DOLORES picks up can on way to kitchen.)

DOLORES. If you need anything, ring the plantation bell and I'll come a-running, Miss Scarlett.

(DOLORES exits.)

SILVA. Last time she ran was when the oven exploded, then she elbowed me off the fire escape. Ouch!
SAM. What's the matter?
SILVA. Bruises; two hours rehearsing a close duet with Shirley Bassey. She nearly had my eye out and for encores, two brutal swipes at my left tit. I am black and blue all over.

SAM. She I presume, is merely black all over.

SILVA. And limping, poor angel. I kicked the wrong way at the finale and nailed her just under the kneecap—we had to finish early.

SAM. You should have come straight home to rest.

SILVA. And miss the lunch for Female Person of the Year Award?

SAM. Christ, I'd forgotten. You didn't win, did you?

SILVA. Be sensible. A lovable, genuine, sincere-type vagina got it.

SAM. Praise be, it would have damaged your image.

SILVA. Silva Ring, the Singing Slut?

SAM. Hardly that ... but you're never going to be the Woman Next Door, are you?

SILVA. I had noticed a serious lack of offers for that position.

SAM. The grass is always greener. Want a drink?

(SAM drains his and goes to replenish it. SILVA sits up.)

SILVA. Why haven't I got one? I drove back with a monkey on my back longing for one.

SAM. You've been too busy moaning. Seldom have I heard such a hard done by little International Star.

SILVA. Don't put me down, Sam; I'm standing on the bottom of the ocean with my nose against the waves.

(SAM hands SILVA's drink and puts hand on her shoulder, gives her a hug.)

SAM. You're tall enough and you're strong enough.

SILVA. Sometimes. How's Jane? Better?

SAM. Still suicidal but alive.

SILVA. And the kids?

SAM. O.K. Sarah's about to drop her first unmarried baby.

SILVA. Don't take it to heart. Hardly any babies are married nowadays.

(DOLORES enters.)

DOLORES. Do you want anything?
SILVA. Privacy.
DOLORES. Can I take the rest of the day off then?
SILVA. No.
DOLORES. Back to de cotton picking.

(DOLORES exits.)

SAM. Who was at the award lunch?
SILVA. The usual lot, sagging guest personalities and glowing anonymous do-gooders.
SAM. Darling, we go back a long way, tell me what turned the day sour.
SILVA. *(Pause.)* Lola Wales.
SAM. Lola Wales is one of you idols! You've bored me silly for years with her old recordings. This bit's marvelous ... if only I could phrase like that ... she's incredible, etc., etc., ad vomit.
SILVA. I know but it was sad meeting her, she was at my table. An old, crumpled Harrods carrier bag. She's tiny and she was dwarfed by this enormous hat. All I could see were small hands smothered in liver spots putting away a few shrimps and endless gin and tonics.
SAM. Lethal combination. Wasn't she fascinating?
SILVA. She was far too plastered, smiled a lot without focus. Her hat fell off at the brandy stage and she soon followed it. I picked her up, took her home and put her to bed.
SAM. Now I get it. The shabby bedsit with dusty souvenirs.
SILVA. Actually no. Regents Park, rather grand. Money signs a plenty. She obviously had a crook with a conscience like you to look after her finances.
SAM. Then why Miss Downbeat?
SILVA. Oh, parallels and things ... what am I talking about?

I looked into a clear crystal ball and saw my final fate. Very encouraging.

SAM. Silva, don't be over dramatic.

SILVA. I cant' help it. Old age is like early death—unacceptable and obscene.

SAM. Look on the bright side, at least you can't suffer both.

SILVA. True.

(SILVA goes and examines her face closely in mirror.)

SILVA. Jawline holding up well ... neck only a minor disaster area ... eyeballs floating like lead pellets in aspic ... excrement, will you look at that?

SAM. What?

SILVA. Are you blind? Round my eyes. Some evil fairy's grafted chicken skin there overnight.

SAM. You're a very attractive woman.

SILVA. Not enough. The world is full of suicidal very attractive women. Have I got time to have a face lift before the T.V. Spectacular? Nothing massive, just a bit of tidying up.

SAM. No, not unless you plan to spend the hour singing, 'Two Lovely Black Eyes' and doing Giant Panda impersonations.

SILVA. Maybe Nico could do something with my hair so only my nose showed, I'm quite fond of that.

(SAM places an arm around SILVA and looks in mirror too.)

SAM. Look at me, I could do covers for the National Geographic.

SILVA. I'm about to be elected Miss Railway Map of Europe. Sam, I've got to do something.

SAM. Trust me, there's no need. And we don't wish to end up like the Iron Duchess, do we?

SILVA. Ah, didn't tell. Saw her last week, she's had even

more work done. The look of permanent surprise has stretched into one of perpetual horror. The skin's tighter than Drake's Drum, you could bounce marbles off it.

SAM. So be warned, no face lifts.

SILVA. No, I'm scared of the knife. Estee Lauder and I will have to soldier on together. Don't go. I'm going to stun myself alive with a quick shower.

SAM. Wait. You've got to see Bergman first.

SILVA. *(Disbelief pause.)* In Casablanca?

SAM. Dr. Bo Bergman, you idiot, he's due any minute. Going to do a piece on you for the big new glossy, Colossus.

SILVA. Excrement, Sam, it's been a hard day. I'm not in the mood for grubby journalists.

SAM. He's a big Viking, Nobel Prize winner and Sweden's most distinguished historian and archaeologist.

SILVA. Fallen on hard times, has he? What was it, drink, drugs or little boys?

SAM. You never bloody listen, do you? I outlined the whole shebang weeks ago. Colossus is the magazine that cuts out the middleman—no journalists. The idea is that celebrities will interview each other. That way we get publicity twice and the public gets a fresh approach. I'm trying to fix it for you to do Mel Gibson.

SILVA. That does sound nice, this sounds deadly and I'm tired, Sam.

SAM. Glitter for ten minutes, that's all I'm asking. *(Door-bell rings.)* There. Vikings are prompt. I'll let him in.

SILVA. Let Dolores answer it—I believe in disconcerting the opposition. I'd better sit with my back to the light.

(SILVA arranges herself on the sofa. DOLORES crosses the stage.)

DOLORES. Are you in now?

SILVA. Only if it's big and blond.

DOLORES. I hope it's Shelley Winters.

(DOLORES exits to lobby.)

BO. *(V.O.)* Good afternoon, Dr. Bergman, I have an appointment.

DOLORES. *(V.O.)* Wipe your feet and follow. *(She is followed into room by big, blond, bearded BO BERGMAN wearing a shapeless tweed suit, forties and amiable as a Labrador. Carries briefcase. Swedish/American accent.)* Miss Ring is resting her varicose veins.

(SAM steps quickly forward and takes BO's hand.)

SAM. Sam Johnson, Silva's manager. It's good to meet at last, Doctor.

BO. Hello.

(SAM ushers BO to SILVA who is 'on show' and extending a long arm.)

SAM. Darling, this is the celebrated Dr. Bo Bergman you've been longing to see.

SILVA. Enchanté.

BO. A great pleasure, Miss Ring.

SILVA. Let's not begin with formality. I'm Silva and you're Bo. Agreed?

BO. Whatever you say, Silva.

SILVA. Good. Now come and sit by me.

(BO sits next to SILVA as DOLORES advances from background.)

DOLORES. And since we're all being so chummy, I'm Dolores.

BO. Hi, it is a beautiful name.

DOLORES. It's Spanish for pain.

SILVA. Yes, dear and we could complete a jolly phrase if

only one of us knew the Spanish for arse. Will you take tea with us, Bo?

BO. The ancient British ritual. Sure thing.

SILVA. Tea for three, Payne.

DOLORES. Yes, Your Honor.

SILVA. And if you could change your attire, I think we would all breathe more freely.

DOLORES. Certainly, Milady. Three bags full, Milady. God Bless Your Worship.

(DOLORES bows out backwards.)

SAM. Ha, Dolores has such a rich sense of humor.

SILVA. She is also partially insane. I employ her chiefly out of kindness and social conscience.

BO. I must tell you that this is a wonderful moment for me. I am a great admirer of yours, Silva. Your concert in Stockholm four years ago was knockout. I play your tapes all the time on my field trips, you are fantastic.

SILVA. *(To SAM.)* He's rather sweet. How long have you been in London?

BO. Three days now.

SILVA. So you've neglected me shamefully.

BO. Not from choice. I had so many meetings with my publishers and publicity for my book.

SILVA. I know, I know—the treadmill of Fame. Do you still enjoy it all?

BO. For me it is a totally new experience.

SILVA. How thrilling! What's your lovely book about?

BO. The Queen of Sheba.

SILVA. Fascinating.

(SILVA is on automatic vamp. BO is getting closer and closer.)

SAM. We were wondering, Bo, how you want to handle this interview? It's an unusual assignment for you.

BO. I can approach it only as an archaeologist, the careful gathering of facts and I hope, a great amount of field research.

SILVA. Essential. But no deep digging, I trust?

BO. That will come as a relief.

SAM. And no camping on the site.

BO. No, I am completely heterosexual.

SILVA. *(Snorts.)* I think Sam meant ... the pitching of tents.

SAM. Most certainly I did.

BO. Ah! Yes hotel rooms are more comfortable though a night under canvas with the wind racing the moon can be a wildly exciting experience.

SILVA. I bet! With the ropes straining and the flaps flapping. Wow!

SAM. Now that you two have melted the ice, can we fix up a timetable?

BO. I'm available anytime till I fly to the States on Sunday.

SILVA. So soon?

SAM. Silva.

SILVA. Mmmmmmmm.

SAM. Check your diary for tomorrow.

SILVA. Sorry.

(SILVA breaks the gaze with BO and goes to diary and flicks pages.)

SILVA. Friday ... Friday ... oh, excrement! Dance class 8:30 ... T.V. rehearsal till noon ... costume fitting ... radio plug, that's a quickie and recorded so we can work round that ... photo session—remember to take linoleum veils ... and dinner with a copulating bore that I intended to cancel anyway.

SAM. Good, so you'll have plenty of time to give Bo what he wants.

SILVA. I'll be well and truly knackered but yes, O.K.

BO. Sounds perfect.

(SILVA stretches and half-twirls in the window.)

SILVA. The river looks lovely and I feel bright again. Hooray!

BO. Silva—the name suits you to perfection. At what age did you change it?

SILVA. By happy chance it's my given name.

BO. *(Laughing.)* You cannot fool me, I'm a researcher. Only this morning I was looking at your birth certificate.

(Small but deadly pause. SILVA freezes. SAM swallows.)

SILVA. It may take some time to get used to your Swedish sense of humor, Bo.

SAM. Ha, was it difficult blowing up the vaults of the Bank of England?

BO. *(Unaware.)* I would not dare. It was the office in Islington, The Family Records Centre.

SAM. The B ... B ... Births Registry?

SILVA. What is this place?

BO. It is where details are kept of the births of all British citizens.

SILVA. Every single detail of every single citizen?

SAM. Yes.

SILVA. For all and sundry to sniff and pry?

BO. They are most helpful towards researchers.

SILVA. What an evil place! Why don't the authorities close it down.

BO. It is an official government department. I have a photostat of your birth certificate, I can show you.

SILVA. Ah! Yes. Please. I'd be intrigued—especially as I was born abroad under exceptional circumstances which force me strongly to doubt its authenticity.

(BO exits to lobby where DOLORES left his briefcase.)

SAM. Shall I leave the room or the country?
SILVA. Don't play silly sodomites.
SAM. It could be the real thing.
SILVA. If it is, you're my manager, you'll have to kill him.

(BO returns pulling photostat from envelope.)

BO. I admit I was amazed. Born in Stratford on the tenth of January nineteen forty-six.

(An immediate crash of broken china from the kitchen arch. SAM is playing with his fingers.)

BO. What was that?
SILVA. Dolores often loses her balance, especially with a doorknob in her ear. Sam, an agent who counts on his fingers does not remain one for long.
SAM. Just a nervous tic.
BO. Now may I reveal your little secret?
SILVA. Can there be more? Am I Hitler's daughter?
BO. Your real name is Iris Elizabeth Ring.
SAM. I am flabbergasted.

(SILVA takes photostat.)

SILVA. How extraordinary. Iris ... what a flood of memories ... Iris. It's a natural assumption on your part, my dear Bo, but nevertheless a confusing not to say slanderous one. The truth is that Iris—
SAM. Was her mother.
SILVA. You really have no head for figures. Iris was ... Iris is ... my beloved sister *(She retreats into childlike introspection.)* Sensible Iris was a second mother to me. Smoothing the way, willing to comfort and guide through any crisis. She called me Spider, I was all arms and legs. How I miss her.
BO. You do not see her now?

SILVA. *(Shakes head.)* We grew apart. Strange, she'd always shared and encouraged my ambitions but the sudden and ridiculous success of 'Silva Ring' frightened her, she was unable to cope with it, regretfully.

SAM. So often happens in this business.

BO. I apologize, I have made an unusual error but I could only find one child born to Arthur and Dora Ring of 13, Andes Crescent, Stratford.

SILVA. That too can be easily explained.

(Pause.)

BO. Yes?

SILVA. Yes. *(She goes to kitchen arch and shouts.)* Dolores! If that fornicating tea's not ready in two minutes flat—we throw you off the Temple precipice at sundown. *(She returns to her window vantage point and speaks in heroic terms.)* Where were we? ... Ah, yes. I was a late child born in the Argentine. My father was manager of a silver mine at the time, hence my name. Shortly after my birth, a series of savage earthquakes razed to the ground the mountain town where I was born, totally destroying the British Consulate and all its records. So Mummy and Daddy, Iris and baby infant me fled to Europe and safety.

SAM. I had no idea.

SILVA. You can't sing the way I do without having suffered, Sam.

(DOLORES enters pushing tea trolley at speed. Normal dress but silver turban. Pours tea a la British Rail.)

DOLORES. Tea's up. Help yourselves to sugar, it poisons the system.

BO. I would so like an English muffin.

DOLORES. Sorry, they're out of season. Only available when there's an F in the month.

(SILVA drifts back to group. DOLORES hands tea to BO.)

DOLORES. Here you are, sir.
BO. Thank you.

(SILVA picks up photostat.)

SILVA. May I keep this as a memento of poor Iris?
BO. Be my guest.
SILVA. You're so kind.

(DOLORES gives cup of tea to SAM. Bedroom door opens and NICKY DONATELLO enters. Cockney footballer of Italian parentage. Good physique. He wears short robe and is drying his hair with a towel.)

NICKY. Bleeding hair dryer's on the blink again.
DOLORES. *(To SAM.)* See what I mean? Legs!
SILVA. Nicky, it's afternoon! You can't still be here.
NICKY. Your lucky day doll. Greetings all.
SAM. Shouldn't you be training, Nicky?
NICKY. No, got this slight groin problem, haven't I?
SILVA. I can vouch for that.
NICKY. Don't slice me up, Sweetheart. You're not so versatile yourself before a gig.
SILVA. A Gig! I only ever give concerts. You're so third class.
NICKY. That's what I love about her, not an ounce of malice. *(He stops DOLORES pushing the tea trolley.)* Any chance of some breakfast, my darling?
DOLORES. Do I have to feed your bit of fluff?
SILVA. Stop making waves, Dolores.
DOLORES. How do you fancy double egg and chips, tea and bread and butter?
NICKY. Lovely.
DOLORES. Good There's a dirty Itie caff down the market.

(DOLORES exits with trolley.)

NICKY. Notice the way she can't keep her eyes off my legs.

SILVA. We're busy, Nicky.

NICKY. *(To BO.)* Ain't had the pleasure, have I? Nicky Donatello.

SAM. Sorry, this is Bo, he's writing a profile on Silva.

NICKY. Anything you want to know, just ask me, Derek.

BO. The name is Bo, it is Swedish.

NICKY. Yeah, it would have to be. Well, I'm off for some grub. Nice meeting you.

(NICKY exits to kitchen.)

SILVA. I'm told he's quite brilliant with his feet.

SAM. Come on, he's one of our leading footballers.

BO. I recognized him from your press cuttings. He's your latest live-in-companion, is he not?

SILVA. No, he's my occasionally stay all night if he's lucky companion.

BO. He looks younger than his photographs.

SILVA. You seem in the grip of an obsession.

SAM. Nicky's ancient in career terms. At thirty most athletes have one foot in the crematorium.

SILVA. Forgive me, chaps, but I'm drop dead tired and I have to show my face and boobs at a film premiere tonight, so ...

SAM. Yes, you put your feet up. I have to get back to the office, can I drop you anywhere, Bo?

BO. I have a car, thank you. *(He kisses SILVA's hand.)* I look forward to tomorrow.

SILVA. Yes, bye.

SAM. I'll see you to the lift.

(SAM and BO exit. SILVA explodes into action, seizes birth certificate and tears it to shreds on coffee table. DOLORES enters at speed behind trolley, throws cups on and attempts to sweep up bits of the certificate.)

DOLORES. What a messy lot.

(SILVA grabs her wrist.)

SILVA. In Saudi Arabia they'd chop your hand off.
DOLORES. I'm only clearing up.
SILVA. Piss off.
DOLORES. *(Retreating.)* I do regret turning down that job with the Duchess of Kent.
SILVA. She thanks God every day.

(DOLORES exits with trolley. SILVA finds crucial bit of paper and eats it. SAM has re-entered, watched her, then comes brightly forward.)

SAM. That went quite well, I thought.
SILVA. That Scandinavian vagina is not to come near me again.
SAM. He's a brilliant man in his field.
SILVA. This old ruin refuses to be poked about.
SAM. He's got a sure-fire best seller out next month. All the inside dirt on how he discovered the tomb of the Queen of Sheba.
SILVA. Oh, yes. And how old has he decided she is, poor cow.
SAM. My voices tell me I'm going to need a drink.

(SAM crosses to drinks. SILVA strides angrily about.)

SILVA. How could you set me up like this? Silva Ring surveyed by archaeologist—the very idea's an inept joke but when he also turns out to be an obsessive little penis waving a birth certificate, it is time to pack it in, mate.

SAM. Give him a chance, he's a simple peasant form the Northern forests—the woodcutter's son.

SILVA. Lovely, he can chop me in half and count the rings.

SAM. He fancies you.

SILVA. He's sex mad, probably got his leg over Sheba's bones. And another thing, I read about that tomb, there were five decoy chambers—the man does not give up easy. He'll be at the British Museum by now, searching for traces of me in the Elgin Marbles or pouring over the parish register for Pompeii!

SAM. We all know that age is a very delicate subject with you but come on, you mustn't allow it to become your Achilles foot and leg, my dear.

SILVA. Yes, make jokes, shake madam out of it. Sam, at this moment, I wouldn't laugh if Barbara Streisand's fornicating nose fell off.

(Short pause.)

SAM. I think I would ... if it dropped off in a public place ... say the Hollywood Bowl ... nothing nasty mind you, just an old rubber one she'd been using for years.

SILVA. *(Hairline crack.)* Sam, I will not be diverted.

SAM. You do look beautiful.

SILVA. When I'm livid?

SAM. And at least fifteen years younger.

SILVA. Thanks. *(Pause.)* What do you mean by fifteen years younger? Fifteen years younger than what?

SAM. Don't know, first number I thought of.

SILVA. You despicable liar. You actually believed that birth certificate was mine, didn't you?

SAM. What, over fifty? That's ridiculous.

SILVA. You've never known my age, nobody does. Even I don't know.

SAM. How come?

SILVA. When I was twenty-one, I hired a hypnotist to erase the memory.

SAM. Have a drink. You need it.

SILVA. Fifteen years younger than whom, Sam?

SAM. Than you sweet sister Iris. Cheers.

SILVA. Strange, I don't recall that you ever met Iris.

SAM. Would you like a tranquillizer.

SILVA. No, why do you ask?

SAM. Politeness. I'm taking two.

(SAM fishes in his pocket and takes pills. SILVA relaxes in chair.)

SILVA. Mind you, Iris did look young for her age. We were very much alike. At dusk, people mistook us for twins.

SAM. I can't believe that, you're unique.

SILVA. Sweet Sam.

SAM. Honest Sam. I believe there's nothing you can't do if you put your mind to it—even twist big Swedish peasants round your little finger.

SILVA. True, I have copes with endless Chat Shows and their parasitic hosts.

SAM. Several deranged record producers.

SILVA. And one film director stroke psychopath.

SAM. So who's this schlemiel, Bo Bergman?

SILVA. Okay, go ahead. I'll find a way. He has incidentally given me the most marvellous idea for Christmas cards.

SAM. Sure you don't want a tranquillizer?

SILVA. Listen, that Births Registry place, I can spend some happy hours in there with a list of maiden names. Get copies of the more devastating certificates, draw a spring of holly on and there's a few ruined seasons of goodwill.

SAM. You won't get many surprises. Everyone's older than their press handouts—except the Queen.

SAM. Now that really is unfair. Every year they force the

poor darling to celebrate the whole thing in public with guns, carriages and horses. I'd sooner die.

(SAM goes to his briefcase.)

SAM. I'll leave the new album sleeve for you to look at and I need your signature on a few things. *(He brings papers and pen to her.)* Where the crosses are.
SILVA. What are these?
SAM. Nothing to worry your pretty head about. Just sign.

(SILVA signs top paper then stops.)

SILVA. I must have a migraine coming on—this appears to be some kind of blank check.
SAM. What! I'll have to get rid of that girl, she's hopeless. Carry on.

(SILVA hesitates then puts pen down and rises.)

SILVA. No, the day is accursed. I make no further move without examining the entrails of an ox. And here comes one now.

(NICKY enters eating a plate of scrambled eggs and sits.)

NICKY. Where's Bo and Arrow got to?
SAM. He flew and so must I. You won't forget the contracts?
SILVA. No.
SAM. Bye, Nicky.
NICKY. See you, Sam.

(SAM exits. SILVA leans over NICKY's chair.)

SILVA. Listen, carefully, lover boy If Bo-Peep tries to pump you about me, play it straight. None of your jolly would-be funny remarks. Capice?

NICKY. Have I ever let you down? I mean, the Press are constantly asking what someone as young and pretty as myself sees in a singer what's been going as long as what you have.

SILVA. Oh, send in the clowns.

(SILVA half strokes the back of NICKY's head and swiftly pushes his face down into the plate of eggs.)
(Curtain.)

Scene 2

(The following afternoon. BO listening to tape recorder.)

(VOICES on tape.)

BO. Why did you never marry?
SILVA. I never thought it necessary.
BO. Have you any children?
SILVA. Not that I know of.
BO. Your own childhood in the Argentine, was it lonely?
SILVA. Never, I had my sister Iris for company. Urination, darling, I promised to call someone. Look after yourself for a moment will you?

(BO turns off recorder and moves upstage to look at framed Gold Discs. DOLORES enters form kitchen. She wears a lurid lurex top under her cardigan.)

DOLORES. Will you be wanting more coffee?
BO. No, thank you. I don't know about Silva though.

DOLORES. Where is she?

BO. Making a call.

DOLORES. Well, she can holler if she does.

BO. It's an impressive collection.

DOLORES. An egocentric's dream. Pure Silva, Silva Blues, Silva Spoons (that dates her), Silva Rocks, Sterling Silva and her's the artwork for her latest, Heigh Ho Silva—a foray into Country and Western.

BO. Why is she wearing a mask?

DOLORES. They say it's the Lone Ranger—I say it's to hide the crow's feet.

(BO switches on recorder.)

BO. How long have you worked for Miss Ring?

DOLORES. Several lifetimes. I am living proof of the theory of re-incarnation.

BO. You must have been very young when you started?

DOLORES. Don't waste your cassette on me dear, 'cause I'm not telling.

BO. I find your loyalty refreshing.

DOLORES. More like self interest. I've written my own memoirs and if Silva kicks the bucket, I shall be peddling many sensational disclosures in the open market.

BO. Is she aware of your work?

DOLORES. I leave the odd page lying about if she gets difficult.

(Doorbell rings. She moves to lobby as SILVA enters from bedroom in a loose, flowing but revealing dress.)

SILVA. Dolores, what are you doing?

DOLORES. Answering the door or hang gliding, take you pick.

(DOLORES exits.)

SILVA. Sorry if I took so long, I decided to ease myself out of my jeans.

BO. It was worth every minute.

(Muffled curses and thumps from lobby.)

SILVA. Are you being mugged, woman?

(DOLORES enters with bunch of florists roses, sucking her thumb.)

DOLORES. I hate roses. They lacerate one.
SILVA. Who sent them?
DOLORES. They're from Wales.
SILVA. Cardiff, Swansea or Save the?
DOLORES. From Lola.

(DOLORES hands card to SILVA.)

SILVA. 'I owe you one. Love Lola.' Quite a steady hand too. How sweet of ... of my grandmother. Don't stand there like a pillar of salt, Payne. Deal with the blooms.

DOLORES. I'll arrange them tastefully in a vase of gin, modom.

(DOLORES exits.)

SILVA. How sweet of the old girl.
BO. It would be of great interest to meet your grandmother.
SILVA. Really? I'll try to arrange it though she doesn't go out much. Shall we go on with the interview?
BO. My tape has run out.

(BO switches off recorder. SILVA goes to hi-fi unit and switches off.)

SILVA. I'd forgotten, mine's still recording. What's the matter?

BO. I'm disillusioned. Today, I thought you trusted me.

SILVA. But I do, Bo. You've been adorable, kept out of the way at the studios, gave me a perfect lunch and steered me through a painless interview. Thanks.

(SILVA gives BO a kiss on the forehead. He points at the hi-fi.)

BO. Then why that?

SILVA. It's ingrained in me. You'd never believe, I've caught journalists bugging my phone, rifling through my handbag, my laundry basket and one fornicating French bastard even hid a camera in the bidet.

BO. But I am different. I am a gentleman.

SILVA. Even so, I barely know you.

BO. Then why don't we go to your bedroom and screw? *(Pregnant pause.)* Well?

SILVA. Sorry, I was just thinking how extra quiet it gets at moments like this but the answer's no, never.

BO. You've encouraged me.

SILVA. Part of the public image.

BO. You have slept with hundreds of men.

SILVA. Partly part of the public image. I happen to be a one man at a time kind of girl.

(BO scatters a sheaf of photographs from his case.)

BO. Here are many press photos of you with your lovers. Athletes, boxers, tennis players, footballers ... acrobats.

SILVA. I have said that sex is my favorite hobby.

BO. And Love?

SILVA. Takes time.

BO. Ha. Certain breaks in the pattern, here you are with Woody Allen.

SILVA. I'd sooner bed the Woody Woodpecker. You'll also come across a picture of me smiling between the Prime Minister and the Archbishop of Canterbury—there's a cozy threesome for you.

BO. So you are merely a sex *symbol*?

SILVA. Be sensible, not even a tom cat could live up to my public image.

BO. My offer of making love was to the private image.

SILVA. Precious stuff, not much of that left.

BO. Sexual relations are a good short cut to getting to know someone.

SILVA. I prefer the scenic route. *(Lightens.)* You don't exactly make it easy; glasses, beard and under that shapeless suit you could be hiding Tarzan or Bugs Bunny.

BO. Stupid of me, I disregard your physique obsession. Of course you wish to see me undressed before reaching your decision.

(BO flings off his jacket.)

SILVA. Wait! Why don't you shave first.

(BO unbuttons his shirt.)

BO. Every day I swim even in our winters.

SILVA. Please, Dolores' book is far too long as it is. *(BO takes off shirt revealing a vest.)* Oh, a vest! I haven't seen one since school. *(BO begins to unbuckle his belt. She rushes to him hands outstretched.)* Stop it. That's quite far enough.

BO. You want to do the rest?

(SILVA is near and facing BO, he draws her to him and kisses her, quite a long kiss then she pulls away.)

SILVA. *(Slow smile.)* You really are a copulating anal orifice. And the answer's still no.

BO. That's better than never.
SILVA. Yes. Yes it is.

(BO picks up his shirt as front door slams and a whistling NICKY in a track suit enters, grins and bounces a football.)

NICKY. Hello hello. Christ, muscles like kippers bollocks.
SILVA. Don't you ever knock?
NICKY. Not when I got keys. Be daft, wouldn't it?
SILVA. What do you want, Nicky?
NICKY. You've forgotten! I knew you had, you're not exactly dressed for kicking a ball, are you?
SILVA. I wouldn't rely on that. What are you talking about?
NICKY. Football practice, darling. Saturday tomorrow, big match for kiddies charities, you promised to appear and kick off.
SILVA. I don't need intensive training for that. I'll give the wretched thing a swift poke and walk off smiling and waving my flowers.
NICKY. You coming tomorrow, Booboo? Pick up a few tips, watch me score?

(BO is dressed and is gathering his case and tape recorder.)

BO. I would like to but I have engaged a detective agency to trace Silva's missing sister and I may have to follow up on any information.
SILVA. What a clever thing, why didn't I think of that?
NICKY. I never knew you had a sister.
SILVA. You're not her type.
NICKY. Stupid is she?
BO. I must go. Thank you Silva for a delightful and interesting day.
SILVA. Why don't we have dinner tonight?
BO. Fine.

NICKY. Suits me.

SILVA. Marvelous. I'll ask Sam and Jane as well. Here for drinks around eight.

BO. Till this evening then.

SILVA. Bye. *(BO exits. NICKY sprawls on sofa.)* Don't make yourself comfortable, I've got work to do.

NICKY. I'm in the mood for a little workout.

SILVA. Tough!

(SILVA goes to unit and looks through tapes. NICKY comes up behind her.)

NICKY. You know when I came in just now, I got the strangest feeling ...

SILVA. Oh, yes.

NICKY. I felt put out ... jealous like.

(SILVA turns and caresses his neck and mouth.)

SILVA. That has to be the nicest thing you've ever said.

NICKY. Crazy. There's no future in it.

SILVA. We never kidded ourselves.

NICKY. Still, let's not waste all this good warm emotion. Come on.

(NICKY breaks embrace and tries to pull her towards bedroom. SILVA detaches herself.)

SILVA. Work. You go and play in the traffic.

NICKY. Sure?

SILVA. *(Nods. He turns to go.)* Nicky ... thanks. *(She turns tape on loud and mimes to her singing, jokingly as NICKY covers his ears and runs out. She picks up address book and punches out a phone number. As an afterthought she turns music off.)* Hello Lola? ... This is Silva, Silva Ring. I wanted to thank you for the gorgeous roses ... Did you mean what you put on the card? ... You said you owed me one ... It's rudely short notice but if you're free this evening, we could wipe the slate clean ... Wonderful, my place seven thirty. I'll explain everything before the others arrive. Bye. *(Puts phone down and shouts.)* Dolores!

(DOLORES appears immediately.)

DOLORES. Your wish is my command, Aladdin.

SILVA. Get Famous Fred the Forger round here fast.

DOLORES. He hasn't finished your driving license—trouble with the ink.

SILVA. I've got a couple of other jobs for him. Oh, and ask him to bring a ground plan of the Family Records Centre.

DOLORES. Anything else?

SILVA. Yes. Tidy up this place, bring the roses in, put a stack of cocktail bits out and make up the bed in the spare room.

(SILVA moves to bedroom.)

DOLORES. Shall I paint the fire escape while I'm at it?

SILVA. Why not?

(SILVA exits to bedroom and re-opens door immediately.)

SILVA. *(Shouts.)* No! Don't you dare touch the fire escape.

(SILVA closes door. DOLORES looks surprised for the first time this year.)
(Curtain.)

Scene 3

(Dusk. Lights beginning to show up across the river. Olives and nuts in dishes. DOLORES enters with vase of roses.)

DOLORES. Bang dat drum and tote dat bale. *(DOLORES catches sight of SILVA coming in from the fire escape wearing a shimmering silver dress.)* Memsahib enjoy the evening cool.

SILVA. There's a fornicating lot of rubbish on the roof. Has Famous Fred gone?

DOLORES. Yes, trembling all over, poor love. Says he's never been asked to pull such a dangerous job.

SILVA. He will be alright?

DOLORES. Course, you can resurrect him quicker than Lazarus by rustling used banknotes.

SILVA. Good. Where's my passport by the way?

DOLORES. I hid it in your Silva Balls C.D.

SILVA. Bells! That doesn't seem very safe to me.

DOLORES. Who's going to want to play that—it's not Christmas.

SILVA. You win. Listen, I want you to play it by ear to-night and keep on your points. I may need fast help and bizarre distractions.

DOLORES. You do know what you're doing?

SILVA. Yes.

DOLORES. I don't know why you bother.

SILVA. Let's forget the concern and philosophy bit, we don't have time. Do you want a drink?

DOLORES. I put one down somewhere. Got it.

(DOLORES finds glass on hi-fi unit. SILVA pours herself a mineral water.)

SILVA. This Swedish phallus is proving harder to shake off than a Readers Digest subscription. So I'm bringing in the family.

DOLORES. Not the dreaded Iris, please, she's hateful.

SILVA. I happen to be rather fond of my sister but I'm keeping her in reserve at present.

DOLORES. Hosannah!

SILVA. This evening's group will be introduced to my dear old grandmother, Lola Wales.

DOLORES. But you'll never get away with it.

SILVA. Why not? Bo won't know who she is. Nicky's too young and ignorant. Jane will be busy mutilating herself and Sam will keep his mouth shut.

DOLORES. What about Lola's mouth?

SILVA. We keep that nicely topped up with gin. Don't overdo it unless it becomes policy for her to crash out.

DOLORES. Wouldn't it be simpler and just as believable for me to tearfully break down and confess that you are my love child, an early peccadillo with King Carol of Rumania?

SILVA. Copulatingly noble of you, loyal retainer. But facts have to be faced—I look far too young for that.

DOLORES. Ow!

SILVA. What's the matter?

DOLORES. Bit my tongue.

(Doorbell rings.)

SILVA. Are your hands working?

DOLORES. Yes.

SILVA. Then open that door. *(DOLORES to lobby.)* Hurry up, she's late as it is.

(LOLA WALES, odd and diminutive under a large hat, appears, takes a step into the room and immediately half falls down. DOLORES and SILVA rush to pick her up.)

SILVA. Heavens Lola, have you hurt yourself?

LOLA. Don't fuss. I'm perfectly alright, I've lined my stomach with milk.

(LOLA lurches and DOLORES and SILVA help her to sofa where she adjusts her hat.)

DOLORES. I'd say the milk was on the turn.

SILVA. Sit quietly and get your breath back. Are you absolutely sure you're okay?

LOLA. Yes, don't go on. You startled me that's all. All that silver, I though you were a robot.

DOLORES. I like your granny.

LOLA. What's the domestic blathering about?

SILVA. I'll explain but first wouldn't you like a small gin and tonic.

LOLA. Not really. But if you're short, it'll have to do.

DOLORES. Not to worry, dear, I'll see you alright.

(DOLORES goes to drinks.)

SILVA. It is good of you, Lola, to come at such short notice.

LOLA. You were a godsend to me at that godawful lunch and there's not much on telly tonight.

SILVA. I struck lucky, then. And you're so bright this evening, you barely spoke a word at the awards.

LOLA. I'd over reached myself; spent the morning courtesy of Berry Brothers, sampling their new wines. Anyway, that's my boring problem. What's yours?

SILVA. Truth is I want a family.

LOLA. If you can't get a man, there's always artificial insemination.

(DOLORES hands LOLA a large gin.)

DOLORES. That alright, Miss Wales.

LOLA. It'll do for starters.

SILVA. Wouldn't you be more comfortable without your hat?

LOLA. Certainly not, it's my barometer.

SILVA. Barometer?

LOLA. Yes, when it falls off, I know I've had enough. *(Throws her head back for a long swig of gin and hat slides sideways.)* Mind you, it's not infallible.

(LOLA shoves hat back on.)

DOLORES. Can I freshen up anybody's drink?

SILVA. That will be all, Dolores.

DOLORES. If you want me just whistle.

(DOLORES exits to kitchen.)

LOLA. Now, my dear, how are we going to get you pregnant? If color's not problem I know this sweet Sikh who would be—

SILVA. Sorry, we don't have much time. The fact is, I want to adopt you.

LOLA. Original!

SILVA. But only for this evening.

LOLA. You're not exactly over endowed with maternal instincts, are you?

(LOLA hold out empty glass which SILVA takes to drinks unit.)

SILVA. Do listen most carefully. I've got this Swedish phallus who's prying into my past and I need a close relative, hopefully you, to confirm some of the stories I've told him. How well do you lie, Lola?

LOLA. Only the truth sticks in my throat.

SILVA. Ha, we could be sisters.

LOLA. Excellent. Tell me about your background now that we've decided I'm to be your sister.

(SILVA brings LOLA's drink.)

SILVA. Well ... er ... that wasn't exactly the relationship I had in mind.

LOLA. Don't ask me to impersonate your brother. I was always hopeless in drag, not like dear old Vesta Tilley or Nelson Eddy.

SILVA. I wouldn't impose on you like that—I just want you to pretend to be my grandmother.

(Pause.)

LOLA. Did you say grandmother—all one word? *(SILVA nods.)* Impossible. I'd have to wear a ton of make-up.

SILVA. Grandma Dietrich not Grandma Moses.

LOLA. Out of the question.

SILVA. I'm afraid my mother's dead.

LOLA. Yet another role beyond my capabilities.

SILVA. I know Aunt. What about Aunt?

LOLA. Your mother's much younger sister?

SILVA. You drive a hard bargain but it's a deal.

(SILVA and LOLA shake on it.)

LOLA. Go ahead, brief me.

SILVA. Born in the Argentine. Parents Arthur and your sister Dora. The crucial member of the Family Ring is your other niece and my sister Iris who is considerably older than I and was born in Stratford in 1946. With me so far?

LOLA. Sounds like some ghastly riddle. But I'm getting the gist.

SILVA. I'll go over it again but if you get totally stuck have a stroke or say you left the deaf aid at home.

LOLA. I have my own routine thanks—amusingly eccentric piss artist.

SILVA. There will be other guests but only worry about the Swede, he's the one— *(Doorbell rings.)* Excrement! What time is it?

(Door slam and NICKY enters.)

NICKY. It's Superstud. Pull you flannel drawers up.

SILVA. What are you playing at?

NICKY. After this afternoon, thought I'd give you a three second warning. Hello, who's this?

SILVA. My beloved Aunt Lola, we're having a private chat.

NICKY. Pleased to meet you, I'm Nicky. Where's Silv been hiding you then?

LOLA. She's been deliberately keeping us apart. I never miss Match of the Day when you're on show, Mr. Donatello.

NICKY. Nice to meet the bright one of the family.

LOLA. Tell me young man, how did you get such lovely thighs?

NICKY. Lots of running around. How'd you get yours?

LOLA. Much the same way.

SILVA. Cold beer in the kitchen, Nicky.

NICKY. Thanks. *(To LOLA.)* Don't you go away, now.

(NICKY collides with DOLORES in kitchen arch, swings her round in full turn and exits. DOLORES continues to lobby without response.)

SILVA. Where are you off to?

DOLORES. I heard the bell.

SILVA. Yes and ignored it.

DOLORES. I'll crouch behind the door all evening if you like. *(Doorbell rings.)* Fast enough for you, Madam?

SILVA. There's a distinct lack of cooperation in the air. *(Savage whisper.)* Oh, and you have no idea where Iris lives.

LOLA. No, no, I don't. Which one is she?

(DOLORES enters followed by SAM in a state.)

DOLORES. Trouble, madam.
SAM. Do I need a drink!
SILVA. Dolores.

(LOLA holds glass on high and DOLORES gathers it on way to drinks.)

SILVA. What's happened? Where's Jane?
SAM. In hospital again. I've just left her.
SILVA. *(Arms around him.)* I am sorry, love. What was it this time?
SAM. Does it matter anymore? Cut her wrists, took the pills and jumped off the Bristol Suspension Bridge, I suppose.
SILVA. They do say it's a cry for help.
SAM. Why can't she do what everybody else does and scream the bloody place down! I'm sorry, I'm going to be useless this evening.

(SILVA gives him extra hug. DOLORES hands out drinks to LOLA and SAM.)

SILVA. There's nothing you can do at the moment. Come and meet Lola Wales.
SAM. I do apologize. I'm a great admirer, Samuel Johnson.
LOLA. Charmed, Doctor.
DOLORES. Would you like a drink, Dolores? Thanks, I'll have a Bacardi and petrol.
SILVA. Lola's divine, she's going to impersonate my aunt and convince the Swedish phallus about Iris.
SAM. Why!
SILVA. Because Iris is vulnerable. He's got detectives hounding her down ...
SAM. So?
SILVA. Iris is a very private person, it could destroy her.

LOLA. Was your mother Flora or Dora?

SILVA. Dora.

SAM. The fact has to be faced, I deliberately surround myself with insane women.

(SAM goes and gazes out of window.)

SILVA. Nicky's convinced.

(NICKY enters with beer and eating.)

NICKY. What about girl?

SILVA. Your crushing beauty.

NICKY. Yeah, I've got a mirror, haven't I? Here, there's some fantastic smoked salmon out in the kitchen.

DOLORES. That's my supper you thieving little toerag.

NICKY. Oh, was it?

DOLORES. I'll break your kneecaps.

(DOLORES rushes out.)

NICKY. Evening, Sam, where's Jane?

SAM. Jane! I haven't rung the hospital.

(SAM rushes to bedroom.)

NICKY. Christ! She' hasn't.

SILVA. She has, poor cow.

NICKY. Can't be any room left—must be cutting her wrists at the elbows.

SILVA. Don't! Come and talk to Lola.

LOLA. Please do, Mr. Donatello. *(NICKY sits next to LOLA.)* Calves like Nijinsky. Lusty peasant legs.

(LOLA pats NICKY's knee.)

NICKY. Go easy on 'em, I got to play tomorrow.

LOLA. I thought the season was over.

NICKY. Charity match at Wembley. Us versus the Krauts.

SILVA. Even I've been roped in to make an appearance.

LOLA. How exciting! Are you going to lead the community singing?

SILVA. No, I'm starting the whole thing off, I hope. It isn't possible to miss kicking a stationary ball, is it, Nicky?

NICKY. You'll be great, I'll lend you my lucky jockstrap.

SILVA. I'm allergic to shellfish. *(Doorbell rings.)* That'll be him.

(SILVA goes to lobby.)

LOLA. Any tickets going for the match?

NICKY. Sure love, one or two?

LOLA. As Mr. Ziegfeld used to say, 'When you visit a liquor store you don't take your own bottle'.

(SILVA enters in high gear with BO.)

SILVA. No, everyone else was fearfully rude and arrived early. Tell me, have your spies managed to trace my sister?

BO. Nothing definite.

SILVA. Never mind, I have a surprise for you. *(She brings him to sofa duo.)* Nicky you know and this is Lola, my favorite Aunt.

LOLA. How do you do?

BO. A pleasure. Aunt? I thought Lola was—

SILVA. A family name, there's one in every generation. Granny couldn't come, she's twisted a Fallopian tube. *(SAM enters from bedroom.)* How's Jane?

SAM. She's recovered. They're letting her loose in the morning.

SILVA. Thank goodness. Get Bo a drink, will you?

BO. Nothing for me.

NICKY. Anyone fancy an olive?

LOLA. I could do with something solid. When's the Swedish phallus arriving?

BO. I can see the family resemblance.

SILVA. This *is* the Swedish fellow.

BO. Tell me, Miss Lola, are you a paternal or a maternal aunt?

SILVA. Lola and Dora were inseparable sisters.

LOLA. Like healthy Siamese twins.

BO. Then presumably you were present at Silva's birth?

LOLA. I drove up to Stratford for it.

BO. I was told the happy event occurred in South America?

SILVA. Quite correct. But there's Stratford on Avon, Stratford Ontario and Stratford on the Andes.

BO. I didn't know that.

SAM. It's odd. Not many people do.

SILVA. Hardly surprising. I'm told their Shakespeare Festival is an absolute copulator.

NICKY. You must have been one of the first women to drive across the Atlantic.

SILVA. Don't be childish, Nicky. She only drove to the airport.

NICKY. Oh, sorry. How long did it take by Zepplin?

SILVA. About the same time it takes to disembowel a footballer.

BO. With such a close family you must have known Iris pretty well?

LOLA. Iris! Did I know Iris! Did I?

SILVA. How it all comes flooding back, the heat of the pampas, the clear mountain air. One of my earliest memories is of being wheeled along in my pram by Aunty Lola with faithful old Iris running merrily alongside.

BO. What was she like?

LOLA. Iris? Oh, an absolutely enchanting dog.

SILVA. Ha, ha, ha. I'd forgotten that old family joke. They did look alike, SISTER Iris hated being teased about it. Sam, Lola's glass is quite empty.

(SAM takes glass for refill.)

NICKY. You want to have a chat with my mum, Bo. She's got a big scrapbook on Silv, been a fan since the flood.
SILVA. What a pity she's pissed off to Sicily. Nuts?

(SILVA thrusts a dish of peanuts at him and contents land in his lap.)

NICKY. Thanks. Was you offering or aiming?

(SILVA moves up to window by fire escape. Joined by BO. They talk. NICKY picking nuts from crotch.)

LOLA. Do you need any help?
NICKY. No, love, I can handle it.

(SAM gives LOLA drink.)

SAM. I went easy on the tonic.
LOLA. I knew you had a kind face.

(LOLA drains drink and sinks back as her hat slides over her face and she sinks into sleep.)

SAM. Goodnight.

(SILVA and BO come arguing from window.)

SILVA. What do you mean Charade! You really are a bore with this obsessive digging into my *(Hoarse whisper croak.)* ancient paaast ... my voice has gone, Sam.

(SAM quickly goes to her.)

SAM. It can't have. The Sunday concert's a sell out.

SILVA. (*Croak.*) Please not too much sympathy.

(*NICKY shouts to kitchen.*)

NICKY. Dolores! The canary's voice box is on the blink. Get the usual crap out.

SILVA. May all your toenails grow in.

SAM. Shut up, don't strain it.

BO. Can I do anything?

SAM. No, Dolores holds a witchdoctor's certificate.

(*DOLORES enters and peers down SILVA's throat.*)

DOLORES. Eeugh! I wouldn't buy that at the butchers. Come on, we'll try a spray but I think it's going to need a paint job.

(*DOLORES leads SILVA towards bedroom.*)

NICKY. I'll sterilize the kitchen knife in case you need to operate.

(*DOLORES and moaning SILVA exit.*)

SAM. If she's not right by Sunday I'm in shtook.

NICKY. Get off! You'll climb into a sequinned frock and mime to her records before you give any money back.

SAM. Last year in L.A. she couldn't sing a note for three days.

NICKY. All singers get hysterical about their pipes. Slightest little thing sets them off.

BO. I think I may have upset her.

NICKY. Pinched her bum did you, Sunshine?

BO. I only asked why she was playing stupid games with me. That old lady is not her aunt at all.

NICKY. Course it's her Aunty Lola.

BO. No, she is Lola Wales, a great blues singer, as good as Billie Holliday in her time. I know because music is my hobby and the chief reason I took on this interview.

SAM. Grow up, digger, the reason you took on this assignment was to do yourself a bit of good. It's called publicity and it sells things, even crappy books about the Queen of Sheba.

BO. You have read my book?

SAM. Don't have to. Great title, fantastic subject, good photographs. A million coffee tables will groan under it.

BO. I only wish to make money so that I can continue my work with total freedom.

SAM. Tell me that again in a year's time, lunching on a yacht, moored off your estate in sunny tax haven land.

BO. I don't think so.

SAM. You'll think more kindly of Silva then. The view is different from inside the machinery.

NICKY. I think the most incredible thing is that Aunty Lola isn't snoring—she looks the type.

(DOLORES makes a quiet and careful exit from bedroom.)

SAM. How bad is it?

DOLORES. Too early to say. I done my best, we'll know more in the morning.

(DOLORES hands SAM a note.)

SAM. *(Reads.)* Sam, sorry to be a bore. Take my forni— my guests to dinner. Booked at the Brasserie.

(Doorbell rings. DOLORES exits to lobby.)

SAM. Shall we go, then?

BO. Sure.

NICKY. There is a small family problem.

(NICKY points at sleeping LOLA. They all look. DOLORES returns followed by IRIS [SILVA without wig, subdued make-up.] carrying an overnight case. Her clothes are neat, simple and unmemorable.)

DOLORES. Kindly wait. Madam is unwell but I'll inform her of your presence.

IRIS. Thank you. *(DOLORES exits to bedroom. IRIS looks at the men and nods.)* Good evening.

NICKY. Hello.

BO. How do you do?

SAM. Good evening.

(They speak softly and stare at her. IRIS looks away then executes the gentlest of double takes and moves awkwardly in sensible shoes to LOLA, raises the hat from her face.)

IRIS. Well, I'm blessed. Aunty Lola!

LOLA. *(Blinking.)* What! ... Where? ... Who the hell are you?

IRIS. You haven't changed. I'm your niece. I'm Iris.

LOLA. Yes, of course, the dog-faced child.

(DOLORES at bedroom door.)

DOLORES. Your sister will see you now, Miss Ring.

IRIS. Thank you, Dorothy.

(IRIS begins to exit towards the bedroom through a frozen tableau.)

(Curtain.)

END OF ACT I

ACT II

Scene 1

(Later that night.
IRIS in high necked candlewick dressing gown and wearing
horn rimmed glasses is sitting at table going over check
stubs, bills and accounts pulled from a filing box. She makes
odd notes and works with a calculator.
DOLORES enters from kitchen carrying tray with two glasses
of milk. She wears multi-colored wrap. She places one glass
on table and moves on.
IRIS speaks without looking up.)

IRIS. Where are you going?

DOLORES. I thought Miss Silva might like some milk.

IRIS. She's been asleep for hours. Leave it here. What's
that you're wearing?

DOLORES. One of Silva's old theatre wraps.

IRIS. It's not suitable for staff. Kindly confine it to your
own quarters.

DOLORES. On my salary one is forced to improvise.

IRIS. I'm glad you mentioned money. Sit down, Dolores.
(DOLORES sits. IRIS pulls sheet of paper from pile.) I've been
going through the accounts to keep myself occupied and to
my slight amazement, your household expenses for the last
year amounted to approximately fifty two thousand pounds.

51

DOLORES. Fancy!

IRIS. I trust you declared most of it as unearned income?

DOLORES. Miss Silva likes to entertain.

IRIS. Given her undoubted talent and unfortunate morals, her social expenses should be nil.

DOLORES. So I keep telling her but the fool clings to independence like a limpet.

IRIS. She's certainly been a very foolish if not downright stupid employer. A few hundred is acceptable as perks for your job, several thousand borders on fraud.

DOLORES. Might you be trying to tell me something?

IRIS. Yes, the party's over. I want everything itemized in future and that means bills, invoices, receipts, loose change and postage stamps.

DOLORES. Most people expect to pay for their little games.

IRIS. That will do, Dolores. Kindly go about your business.

DOLORES. As your ladyship pleases. *(She gets up with a bob.)* How long do you plan to stay this time?

IRIS. Why on earth should that concern you?

DOLORES. The wear and tear on my nerves.

IRIS. You do surprise me. I would expect you merely to raise one over plucked eyebrow were you to be repeatedly raped by Guy the Gorilla.

DOLORES. The family resemblance is uncanny.

IRIS. We are sisters.

DOLORES. Of course, what about a bonus?

IRIS. You'll find me more than fair if you carry out your duties to my satisfaction.

DOLORES. There's bound to be a lot of extra running about and my verucas and fallen arches will crucify me. I gave the best years of my life to the Ballet Rambert.

IRIS. I never knew that. Did you dance major roles?

DOLORES. Occasionally. I wasn't quite good enough but I had my triumphs in supporting parts. Dame Marie shed a tear when I left.

IRIS. Extraordinary! Do you believe in coincidence, Dolores?

DOLORES. Sometimes. Why?

IRIS. Only last week whilst browsing in a secondhand bookshop, I came across a whole pile of old Ballet Rambert programs.

DOLORES. They must have been ... interesting.

IRIS. They were, very. Your name was in every single one. Dorothy Payne, Assistant wardrobe Mistress!

(Pause.)

DOLORES. You Bastard! You rotten, low-down bastard.

IRIS. I've obviously touched an exposed nerve so I'll pretend I didn't hear that.

DOLORES. Nobody has a monopoly on fantasy, nobody.

IRIS. I know. But how foolish to leave the truth so far behind.

DOLORES. I wasn't addicted like some. My dancing dreams were harmless pleasures. Now, nothing won't never be the same again. No never, nevermore.

IRIS. Don't be so negative, woman. Pull yourself together. Apart from me nobody knows or I suspect, cares.

DOLORES. You had no need to, you had no right.

IRIS. If it's any consolation, I'll give you solemn word that I won't tell Silva. *(DOLORES stares hard.)* Well?

(DOLORES kneels and grabs her hand.)

DOLORES. Thank you, bless you. Can I kiss your ring, Your Holiness?

IRIS. That'll do, we'll talk further in the morning. Wake me at seven with a cup of tea and a digestive biscuit.

DOLORES. Seven o'clock! Hardly seems worthwhile going to bed. Goodnight, Madam Iris.

IRIS. Goodnight.

(DOLORES goes to kitchen arch and turns.)

DOLORES. Oh, by the way, what time should I wake Miss Silva?

IRIS. I think we let her sleep as long as she can. There's a lot to be done.

(They hold each other's gaze then DOLORES shrugs.)

DOLORES. If you say so, Herr Commandant.

(DOLORES exits. IRIS tidies paper, she rubs her neck in a gesture of tiredness and gets up to look at the river, sipping her milk. Noise from lobby and NICKY enters in expansive mood.)

NICKY. What an evening! What a giggle, none of them are sure about you. You deserve an Oscar, girl. It was magic, sheer magic. How'd you do it?

IRIS. I've seen you before somewhere. Those crude features are vaguely familiar.

NICKY. No, don't start again, please. I'll wet myself laughing.

IRIS. Yes, of course, one of the pathetic hangers on. What do you want?

NICKY. The usual.

(As NICKY leers at IRIS, she pulls the dressing gown close to her throat.)

IRIS. Drink and drugs, I suppose.

NICKY. Nah, you know how I like to relax before a match. Nice and slow, eh?

IRIS. If you don't leave at once I shall be forced to ring for the police.

NICKY. Oooh! That snotty voice. I like, I like it!

(NICKY advances, IRIS retreats.)

IRIS. I'm warning you, stop!
NICKY. I don't think I can. That terrible dressing gown's a real turn on.

(NICKY places one hand behind IRIS's neck and with the other he attempts to pull the gown apart. She economically knees him and he doubles over.)

NICKY. Jesus! A couple more inches, I'd have been on the substitute's bench for life.

(IRIS picks up the phone.)

IRIS. I'm dialing 999.
NICKY. Don't bother, I won't be preferring charges.

(NICKY stumbles to a chair. IRIS replaces the receiver.)

IRIS. Wait a minute. How did you get it?
NICKY. Flew in the window like bleeding Peter Pan.
IRIS. I'm not putting up with this. Give me the keys immediately.
NICKY. Putting up with what?

(NICKY is rubbing his groin slowly.)

IRIS. Foul mouthed, uncouth animals crashing in at all hours—will you please stop making those obscene gestures. I really don't know what Silva thinks she's at.
NICKY. Bugger me, nor do I.

(IRIS thumps NICKY.)

IRIS. How dare you use that sort of language in front of a lady!

NICKY. Begging your pardon, I thought we was alone. *(IRIS thumps NICKY harder.)* Ow! What's got into you for chrissake?

IRIS. Be quiet or you'll wake her.

NICKY. Fat chance. Dolores will have half a crate of beer down her by now.

IRIS. I was referring to my simple minded sister, Silva.

NICKY. Silva! You got concussion, mate.

IRIS. I do find your style of conversation difficult to follow, Mr. ... er?

NICKY. Lost your voice again, have you? Nicky's the name, Nicky Donatello.

IRIS. What a relief, that explains all. You're foreign

NICKY. Yeah, Soho Italian. You wanta some black peppa?

IRIS. Watch my lips closely. Per favoure, getta losta.

NICKY. I'm going to see Silva.

(NICKY gets up. IRIS bars the way.)

IRIS. That's out of the question.

NICKY. Thought it might be.

IRIS. She has a severe throat infection.

NICKY. You take the message for her. Tell her to recover fast. Tomorrow's one of the most important days of our lives.

IRIS. How dramatic. I sincerely hope that doesn't mean the pair of you intend to be married?

NICKY. Don't make me laugh. My wife's going to be a virgin.

IRIS. Permanently, I presume.

NICKY. What the hell are you implying?

IRIS. Sisters do exchange little secrets.

NICKY. Oh yes?

IRIS. Nothing of any impotence ... I say, I'm most awfully sorry.

NICKY. You bitch! If she's still harping on about last Tuesday, it was entirely her own—

IRIS. Please, please. Silva did not refer to any sordid, specific date.

NICKY. That makes it worse. A blanket allegation like that could ruin my image—gays would start writing me fan letters.

IRIS. Kindly control yourself.

NICKY. It's diabolical. She's had no cause for complaint and she's only one of three I've got on the go at the moment.

IRIS. Do relax, have a drink, kick a cushion round the room. Anything to stop you waving your tiny macho between two fingertips.

(A pause while NICKY glares at her then goes for his belt.)

NICKY. You've done it now. Get the tape measure out.
IRIS. *(Shouts.)* Dolores!

(DOLORES leaps on stage instantly.)

DOLORES. Yes?
IRIS. Hyper-efficiency all of a sudden.
DOLORES. I happened to be passing. What do you want?
IRIS. Merely checking on your availability.

(Doorbell rings.)

IRIS. Good heavens. See who that can be, will you?

(DOLORES to lobby. NICKY pours himself a stiff drink.)

NICKY. You burn up a helluva lot of energy in a football match, did you know that?

IRIS. It's another world; people calling in the middle of the night.

NICKY. Only half past twelve.

IRIS. In Torquay where I come from, that is considered the hour before dawn.

(DOLORES enters with SAM.)

DOLORES. Would your guests care for some cocoa, madam?

IRIS. Thank you no, these gentlemen won't be staying.

SAM. Am I glad to hear your voice.

(DOLORES exits.)

IRIS. And who might you be—another freeloader?

SAM. You know me, Sam ... Sam Johnson.

NICKY. Make her happy, say Napoleon.

IRIS. Mr. Johnson ... ah, yes, Silva's manager. How fortuitous, I intended to telephone you first thing in the morning. You may stay. Goodnight, Mr. Mortadella.

NICKY. There's a couple of things I'd like to get straight first.

IRIS. Please be brief.

(IRIS goes to record shelf and gets her passport.)

NICKY. Sam, have you seen this woman before?

SAM. Yes. I saw her when she arrived.

NICKY. And you honestly believe she's Silva's long lost sister?

SAM. I don't have positive proof but ... well, you've only got to look at her.

NICKY. Exactly. I'd like to see them both stretched out on twin beds myself.

IRIS. Another pathetic male fantasy.

(IRIS drops passport on floor near NICKY.)

NICKY. I got three deals coming to the boil. An advertising contract for aftershave and suchlike, 'My Sensational Lovelife with Silva Ring' in four sizzling installments and most important a good contract with a Spanish club.

SAM. So a lot of good coverage will help clinch the deals and send your price up a bit.

NICKY. Knew you'd understand, Sam.

IRIS. Yes, you have Greed in common.

(IRIS kicks passport to NICKY's feet.)

NICKY. I'm pushing thirty, love. I can see the end of the road and I don't fancy running the provincial pub so I'm cashing in for all I'm worth.

IRIS. I'm curious, do you have any feelings at all towards my sister?

NICKY. Course I have, she's a good sort and a good lay. We've always been honest with—

(NICKY sees passport and picks it up, gives a cursory glance and smiles broadly.)

IRIS. What's that?

NICKY. The jackpot! Silva's passport which she can have back if she shows up at tomorrow's jamboree—if not the tabloids get it.

SAM. That's blackmail!

NICKY. I calls it insurance. Well, what do you say, Sis?

IRIS. I remains convinced that my brave sister would never succumb to threats no matter what the cost, therefore it is with total confidence that I say to you on her behalf publish, publish and be damned.

SAM. Ahem ... Silva has on occasion been reticent about her age.

IRIS. Mr. Donatello and the yellow press will soon settle that.

SAM. Silva will go raving mad. Let's talk this over.

NICKY. *(He waves passport at IRIS.)* I'm not kidding.

IRIS. Neither am I, scumbag! Hand over the keys to this flat and go.

(NICKY hesitates and then gives the keys with bravado.)

NICKY. Cheers, then. Must get to a photostat machine.

(NICKY swaggers out. SAM abruptly gets up.)

SAM. That's sobered me up. I need a drink.

IRIS. I'll join you. There's a bitter taste in my mouth.

SAM. Brandy?

IRIS. Heavens, no. A drop of medium sweet sherry. *(SAM stares with amusement but pours.)* Underneath all the common charm and bravado that young mad is sadly desperate.

SAM. Somehow you panicked him. Not like you at all.

IRIS. How would you know?

(SAM hands IRIS her drink.)

SAM. Drink up.

(IRIS sips delicately.)

IRIS. Delicious, thank you.

SAM. *(Laughs.)* You have just won the Distillers Oscar for the year's best performance with a drink. I love you.

IRIS. What's the matter with this town? Now, you're becoming over familiar.

SAM. It's a great act but you've forgotten one thing. I know Lola ain't Aunty Lola yet those were the first words "Iris" spoke.

IRIS. I see, so you assumed ... Mr. Johnson, I loathe being

party to deception. However, when I arrived in London *(Glances at watch)* ... yesterday, I telephoned my sister as a matter of course. Silva sounded distraught, begged me to come at once and pleaded with me to acknowledge a drunken old lady as our aunt. Knowing nothing of the circumstances, what could I do but agree?

SAM. Oh!

IRIS. Blood is thicker than water.

SAM. And makes rotten ice cream.

IRIS. Pardon?

SAM. Sorry, a private joke I share with Silva ... who will not I fear be amused to hear that Nicky has her passport.

IRIS. They'll be able to do a trade.

SAM. A trade?

IRIS. An exchange. She burbled something about getting hold of a stack of birth certificates including Nicky Donatello's which much to her delight proves he's a couple of years older than he claims to be.

SAM. Really? That could damage his football contract.

IRIS. It's all so much humbug. Why does Silva insist on concealing her age? Thirty nine isn't old nowadays.

(SAM has a small coughing fit.)

SAM. No, no it isn't. Mind you part of Silva's success does depend on the way she looks ... and behaves. All sex symbols attempt to stop time.

IRIS. Something I shall never understand.

SAM. You yourself are very lucky, you don't look any-where near forty ... six.

IRIS. That's because I'm over fifty.

(IRIS begins to laugh softly.)

SAM. What is it?

IRIS. You. Imagining that I was Silva pulling some elaborate hoax. Ha., ha, ha, if she wasn't poorly, I'd wake her to share the joke.

(SAM rises.)

SAM. We can all three get hysterical in the morning. I'll be dropping by, we have some business to transact.

(IRIS picks up a bunch of papers.)

IRIS. I have it here.
SAM. Good, she remembered to sign.

(SAM holds his hand out. IRIS slowly tears papers in half and places the pieces in his hand.)

SAM. What are you playing at?
IRIS. I work for a solicitor in Torquay. I know a rip-off when I see one.
SAM. Miss Ring, the entertainment world is a highly specialized field not readily understood by outsiders.
IRIS. I said Torquay not Tierra del Fuego.
SAM. Silva has trusted me absolutely for the last twenty years.
IRIS. She's been a fool about money all her life.
SAM. With my guidance and protection she's become a millionairess.
IRIS. And you?
SAM. I'm not on the breadline either.

(IRIS sifts through the file.)

IRIS. It's a bewildering mosaic of companies you've set up, mainly with you or your wife as majority shareholders.
SAM. There are tax reasons. How can I explain it to a lay person? It's like an iceberg, the tip you see is the big record-

ing star, below is the huge mass of humble folk and companies that sustain and make the whole thing possible. The cost of that support is astronomical.

IRIS. I understand all that. I'm merely questioning your exceptionally large slice of the cake and odd details such as where does the interest vanish from large capital sums deposited in the Cayman Islands, no trace of any payments for radio plays and the sheer penny pinching of making her finance the flat in Dolphin Square where you entertain young uniformed gentlemen once or twice a week.

SAM. *(Shaken.)* Nobody knows about that.

IRIS. Presumably, several hundred young servicemen do.

SAM. How did you find out?

IRIS. Does it matter?

SAM. Yes, it bloody does.

(IRIS Picks up SAM's glass.)

IRIS. Have another. Must be hard when walls turn to glass. Or I have smelling salts in my case, if you prefer?

SAM. Who told you?

IRIS. No cause for alarm. Some dear friends of mine have a handsome sailor son who on occasion spends his leave in this big wicked city.

SAM. And?

(IRIS hands SAM a brandy.)

IRIS. Sip it. Would you like a blanket to keep you warm?

SAM. NO! ... Thank you.

IRIS. You don't look well.

SAM. Neither does a butterfly wriggling on a pin. Tell me about the sailor.

IRIS. Oh, yes. Well, a couple of months ago on the eve of his marriage, he drunkenly experienced a belated rush of conscience and confessed all to an understanding older woman, me. The whole scene was rather sweet and Tennessee Williamsish.

SAM. How did he know my name?

IRIS. He saw your credit cards when he accidentally opened your wallet. He's always followed Silva's career so he made the connection.

SAM. I see. In this particular area, Blackmail is rather old hat.

IRIS. And quite unthinkable. Mind you, aren't the Armed Forces exempted from the act?

SAM. I wouldn't dream of turning any of them in.

IRIS. You should cultivate that streak of generosity, Mr. Johnson. Wouldn't it be nice if you were to draw up a new personal contract for Silva?

SAM. I'm a sentimental fool. I'm very fond of the old one.

IRIS. Cultivate Sam, cultivate.

SAM. The existing agreement has several years to run.

IRIS. But would they be happy years for you? ... For you, Jane and the family?

(DOLORES enters.)

DOLORES. Can I swab the decks down?

IRIS. Yes, I was on the point of retiring. Would you kindly see Mr. Johnson out?

DOLORES. I'll put him out with the cat, Captain.

(IRIS exits to bedroom. DOLORES puts glasses on tray.)

SAM. Dolores, old chum ... that creature, that monster is Silva, isn't she?

DOLORES. I work for Miss Ring and I'm too old to dance again.

SAM. On the other hand, how did she get out of the bedroom and appear at the front door?

DOLORES. We'll get burgled one of these days. So easy.

stairs by the lift, across the roof and down the fire escape.

SAM. Or vice versa.

DOLORES. You said it, not me.

SAM. The important thing is her state of health, we must call her doctor immediately.

DOLORES. Leave it alone, Sam. She may well have vanished by the time he gets here. Iris doesn't hang round, it's the one bearable thing about her.

SAM. You mean she's done this before?

DOLORES. Three times that I know of.

SAM.   Then we must do something to help her. She's seriously ill!

DOLORES. Iris will go when everything is settled to her satisfaction.

SAM. I don't think that's possible. God, she's powerful. Look at my hands, they're shaking.

DOLORES. Don't expect tea and sympathy, dear. It serves us both right.

SAM. I haven't done anything.

DOLORES. Iris only comes out of the woodwork when Silva's unhappy and feels she can't cope no more.

SAM. What's she got to be unhappy about?

DOLORES. Lots by the sound it. Here, you got a cleaner for your Dophin Square love nest?

SAM. Christ! I'd forgotten eavesdropping was your hobby.

DOLORES. I can easily slip over a couple of afternoons a week and keep the place shipshape.

SAM. No thanks, I don't want it wired for sound.

DOLORES. Suit yourself.

SAM. When was the last time Iris ... manifested herself?

DOLORES. Remember Leo, the mad Polish acrobat?

SAM. I'll say. He was bit heavy.

DOLORES. Silva couldn't get rid of him but Iris went to the Home Office one morning, got a deportation order and Leo and his trapeze were flying out the country by dinnertime.

SAM. She obviously stops at nothing.

DOLORES. And nothing stops her. It's safer to surrender.

(Bedroom door slowly opens. A loud yawn. SAM takes a step back. SILVA enters blinking, wearing wrap, speaking drowsily.)

SILVA. What time is it?
DOLORES. One o'clock in the morning.
SILVA. Funny, I feel as if I'd slept for days.
DOLORES. I didn't say which morning.
SILVA. What! No, I can't have—
SAM. It's alright, darling. It's only Saturday, just.

(SILVA sits.)

SILVA. Thank Heavens. Sam! What are you doing here?
SAM. I popped in to see how you were.
SILVA. Sweet. I don't know, I feel disoriented but beautifully relaxed.
DOLORES. Can I get you anything?
SILVA. Cup of tea would be lovely, if your feet are up to it.
DOLORES. Tiffin for memsahib coming up.

(DOLORES exits to kitchen.)

SAM. Had an interesting chat with your sister.
SILVA. Did you?
SAM. She's not pleased with your contracts.
SILVA. Iris is a perfectionist.
SAM. She knows sod all about the music business. And besides it's bad policy to allow relatives to shove their noses into—
SILVA. Please Sam. I don't mean to push you out but I can't take in a word you're saying. Do you mind, angel?
SAM. Sorry, stupid of me. You get a good night's rest, love. *(Kisses her cheek.)* See you at Wembley Stadium.

SILVA. Don't! I'm dreading the whole thing. Do I have to wear that sodding cowboy outfit?

SAM. Push the product. Heigh Ho Silva will be on sale at all good record shops on Monday.

SILVA. Well, I'm not putting the Lone Ranger mask on, plays havoc with the eye make-up.

SAM. Okay. Sleep well.

(SAM exits. SILVA blows him a kiss then fully alert goes to phone.)

SILVA. Wake up, Famous Fred ... it's Miss Ring, Queen of the Mob. I've got another job for you so get your miserable, pinched arse over here, NOW.

(SILVA grabs paper, pens, London Atlas from shelves and throws them on sofa. DOLORES enters with cup of tea.)

DOLORES. What's going on? Have the Chinese landed?

SILVA. Dump that. I want coffee, lashings of it. We're going to be up all night, planning.

DOLORES. If you don't get no sleep, you're going to look seriously rough in the morning.

(SILVA removes wig.)

IRIS. Kindly do as I say, Payne.

DOLORES. Err ... Yes, Your Majesty.

(Curtain.)

Scene 2

(Late Saturday afternoon. DOLORES talking on phone. She sports silver shoes and big earrings.)

DOLORES. I don't know any more than you do, Nigel, I only saw it on television ... yes, an exclusive item, I promise ... and double my usual fee for this one, Nige ... Right, bye. *(Phone down and it rings at once.)* ... no comment. *(Slams phone down and it rings.)* What now? ... No, Miss Ring cannot take a person to person call from Munich ... I don't care if it's Hitler, dear, she's not in. *(Phone down it rings.)* ... I'm not wearing any ... Time waster! *(DOLORES takes phone to unit and turns answering machine on.)* Enjoy the recorded message. I'm getting cauliflower ears. *(FRED has edged into view along the fire escape. He taps on window with a bandaged hand, winces and changes hands. DOLORES wheels round.)* Aaarh! You stupid sod. You frightened the knickers off me. *(She opens window and drags him in.)* What are you doing out there?

FRED. There's police down the entrance holding a big crowd back.

DOLORES. Worried sick I was. Had your bail money ready all day. Where've you been since this morning?

FRED. Down the hospital. Got severe burns, didn't I?

DOLORES. Lord! Was it the package Miss Iris gave you?

FRED. Five minutes she said I'd have to get clear—two bleeding seconds and the whole place flared up. *(Waves bandaged hand.)* My entire career may be ruined.

DOLORS. You're insured aren't you?

FRED. Forgers and petty thieves don't have the same facilities as bleeding concert pianists, not in this rotten capitalist society.

(Voices in lobby. DOLORES gestures FRED off to kitchen.)

SILVA. *(V.O.)* Perfectly sweet of you officer, of course I'll come to your ball.

SAM. *(V.O.)* Much appreciated, thank you Sergeant.

(SILVA erupts into the room before SAM. She wears cowboy boots, a Stetson, a raincoat (Underdressed for IRIS) and dark glasses. She is high, high, high.

SILVA. I am the Champion, I am the Champion. Did you see it, Dolores? Did you see me score the goal?

DOLORES. I couldn't believe it.

SILVA. The whole fornicating stadium exploded, they yelled easy, easy, eeeeeeasy.

SAM. Why don't you ease up a bit, Silva. You're wildly over-excited.

SILVA. Rubbish! Just being my natural, wonderful, ebullient self. I am the Champion!

DOLORES. It looked like trick photography on the telly.

SILVA. Oh yes, a lot of spoilsports like you waffled on about a freak gust of wind carrying the ball into the net. Utter garbage! I'm a superb natural athlete and that was the best fornicating kick that's ever been. Michael Owen eat your heart out.

(SILVA has been racing around the stage with manic energy, kicking cushions, throwing the Stetson, striking attitudes.

SAM. Pity you had to score for the Germans.

SILVA. Weren't they sweet the way they hugged and kissed me? I take back everything I've said about the Krauts. Dolores, did I see Fred lurking into your quarters?

DOLORES. Yes.

SILVA. Good, I want a quick word with him. Pop the corks, let the champers flow. Heigh Ho Silva!

(SILVA exits to kitchen.)

DOLORES. Has she taken something?

SAM. No, she's ill dammit. I've spoken to Jane's psychiatrist. He's coming here to treat or to certify her.

DOLORES. As bad as that?

SAM. Fraid so. I filled him in on Iris and he said she was in deep trouble. In a high manic state, total absence of any self criticism or self doubt. She thinks she can do anything and up to a point, she can. She's already kicked half the length of a football pitch and she conducted part of the press conference in German and Japanese.

DOLORES. She has sung songs in those languages.

SAM. Lyrics she learned parrot fashion. This afternoon she was swearing and cracking jokes with the foreign press and generally behaving like the Empress of the Universe.

DOLORES. How does it end?

SAM. Collapse. Finally the body won't be able to stand what the runaway brain demands of it.

DOLORES. Poor love.

SAM. I'll have to cancel Sunday's concert though apparently in this condition she could do three or four on the trot. *(Doorbell rings. SAM goes.)* I hope that's Dr. Barnaby now.

DOLORES. There won't be white coats and horrors, will there Sam?

(SAM enters followed by BO with brown envelope.)

SAM. Silva's suffering from stress, it might be better if ...

BO. I leave early tomorrow.

(SILVA enters from kitchen.)

SILVA. Who was that? Bo, darling, how lovely. We're having a party. *(She embraces him.)* Champagne, Dolores, buckets of it.

DOLORES. I'll put some on to chill.

(DOLORES exits to kitchen.)

BO. I leave for New York in the morning, I dropped by to say my good-byes.

(SILVA takes large envelope from BO.)

SILVA. And you brought me a present, how sweet.

BO. No, that is my article on you, I am taking it to the magazine editor.

SILVA. No need, I'll deliver it. Anything I don't like, I'll re-write. *(She shoves envelope in drawer of table/desk.)* And I won't hear of you going before my concert. Sam, cancel his flight.

SAM. Will do.

(Doorbell rings. SILVA is quick off the mark.)

SILVA. The party's getting bigger!

SAM. Please agree with everything she says, no matter how bizarre.

SILVA. *(V.O.)* I am the Champion, I am the Champion.

NICKY. *(V.O.)* Highly comical I'm sure.

(NICKY enters with SILVA baiting him with imaginary kicks.)

NICKY. I could kill you easy.

SILVA. Easy, Eeeasy, eeeeaasy!

NICKY. You can't resist center stage, can you? It was supposed to be my day for publicity.

SILVA. And didn't you get plenty?

NICKY. Yeah, but not in my own right.

SILVA. I just pray and hope someone got a picture of you when I scored—jaw down to the groin darling. *(Doorbell rings.*

SILVA goes.) Probably an offer to play for England ... or Germany!

NICKY. She's bloody raving mad.

SAM. Yes, she is. Don't rile her, Nicky, for God' sake. Do everything she asks.

NICKY. What you talking about?

(SILVA enters supporting LOLA who sports large Ascot hat and man-sized tracksuit.)

SILVA. Take it nice and easy, don't rush.

LOLA. I never suspected that water could taste quite so filthy.

NICKY. I keep telling you, it was soapy, dear. She fell head first into the players' tub, wouldn't you know.

SILVA. You poor soul, did you hurt yourself?

(SILVA helps LOLA into chair.)

NICKY. No, she had total relaxation, pissed as a fart. Three of my mates pulled muscles scrambling to get out of the pool. I'm not very popular at my club.

LOLA. A pint of gin please, Landlord.

SILVA. See to it, will you, Sam?

SAM. Yes, yes of course Silva. Anything.

(SAM hurriedly gets drink.)

LOLA. I want to drink a toast to your winning goal.

SILVA. It was brilliant, wasn't it? Eeeasy, eeasy!

NICKY. Never should have been allowed. Bloody French referee.

SILVA. He was so gallant, I take back everything I've said about the Frogs. He practically ate my hand and whispered, 'Vive la difference'.

(SAM gives LOLA her drink and as he passes NICKY whispers.)

SAM. Be nice.

NICKY. Actually, things haven't turned out too bad. I'm signing for Valencia, Monday and we should hit all the front pages with today's shenanigans. Glad you came to your senses and showed up, Silva. Guess you'd better have this back.

(NICKY hands out her passport which she grabs.)

SILVA. How did you get a hold of this?

NICKY. Your big sister gave it to me.

SILVA. You thirty year old copulating liar.

NICKY. Who are you calling thirty?

SILVA. Ha! I have proof positive, all down in black and white—Nicholas, Alessandro, Gonzalez, Bertorelli, Donatello.

NICKY. How do you know that?

SILVA. Iris happened to be browsing in the Births Registry.

BO. Did you hear, someone started a fire there today?

SAM. Deliberately?

BO. Yes, quite a professional job.

SILVA. I'm only surprised it hasn't been done before. Temples of evil should be destroyed ... Razed to the ground ... All records destroyed ... New beginnings for ... for everyone ... All live happily ... ever ... ever ... evermore ...

(SILVA staggers slightly and holds her head. SAM puts arm round her.)

SAM. We're supposed to be celebrating. Where's the champagne?

SILVA. Yes. Do light the fuse on Dolores. I must go and change out of this stupid, pointless outfit.

(SILVA exits unsteadily.)

SAM. She's beginning to wind down. I wish I knew what happens next.

BO. Should I go, Sam? Get out of the way.

SAM. No, she wants you here. Stay till the doctor comes.

NICKY. Look, what is going on?

SAM. Silva's sick, she's about to flip her lid.

NICKY. Never. It's adrenalin, she often gets hyped up like this.

SAM. You didn't see her with the Press. She's over the edge this time, worse than my wife.

BO. Does she take cocaine?

SAM. She's always been frightened of drugs, thank God.

LOLA. Gentlemen! *(They all turn to look and she hold up her glass.)* My glass is vacant.

SAM. The champagne will be here any minute.

LOLA. Champagne has no bite. French filth, I stick to gin.

BO. I'll give her the bottle.

(BO takes bottle to LOLA and pours.)

NICKY. And a straw to go with it.

SAM. Where's that bloody Dr. Barnaby got to?

(SAM picks up the phone. DOLORES enters pushing trolley with champagne in ice bucket.)

DOLORES. Want me to open it, Sam?

SAM. Not yet. Go and see what state she's in first.

DOLORES. Do you think I should?

SAM. Yes.

(DOLORES goes to bedroom door but as she tentatively goes to knock it is opened by figure in IRIS's clothes and horn rimmed glasses but SILVA's wig slightly askew.)

IRIS. Silva has succumbed to the most frightful migraine. Frankly I'm not surprised the way she's been charging about all day, over excited and over tired like a spoiled child. She's asked me to make her excuses.

(Everyone frozen in horror. SAM replaces phone in slow motion. IRIS goes to BO hand outstretched.)

IRIS. Dr. Bergman, I presume. Silva's told me so much about you. I'm Iris, her sister.
BO. How do you do?

(IRIS moves on to DOLORES by ice bucket.)

IRIS. As it's a special occasion I will break my rule of no alcohol before sundown. Jump to it, Dolores, total paralysis does not become a domestic. You may serve the bubbly.
DOLORES. *(Loud whisper.)* The barnet.
IRIS. I beg your pardon?
DOLORES. *(Louder whisper.)* Wrong wig, Madam.

(IRIS's hand casually creeps up by her ear and she lightly pushes her hair back.)

IRIS. The wrong wig? What business is it of yours? I merely happen to be trying on one of my sister's wigs. Silva is always telling me that I don't make enough of myself so I thought I'd experiment. Obviously a flop judging from your horrified faces. Mutton dressed as lamb, I suppose.

(Pause.)

SAM. Don't you think you should sit down and rest ... Iris?
IRIS. Certainly not. I've had a very lazy day, Mr. Johnson.
BO. You do look a little tired.
IRIS. Age catching up with me, I'm afraid. Despite my

resemblance to Silva ... I do happen ... somewhat old ... older than ... I ... I

(NICKY goes and takes her hands.)

NICKY. Stop it! You don't have to do his. We all care for you, Silva.

(IRIS pulls away and laughs.)

IRIS. Silva! Always Silva! You still think ... this time she has to be told.

(IRIS moves towards bedroom.)

SAM. Stay and have a drink. You know Nicky—no, no you don't but he likes to play the fool.
DOLORES. Wait.

(IRIS exits.)

SAM. God knows what damage you've done, you idiot.
NICKY. I couldn't bear it. I'm fond of the old cow.
BO. She needs professional treatment fast.
SAM. That's what we're waiting for, stupid.
LOLA. I'm well in with Betty Ford.
DOLORES. Aren't you a doctor?
BO. Of philosophy.
DOLORES. Fat lot of good. Sorry I asked.

(Bedroom door opens and IRIS without wig appears.)

IRIS. Could someone draw the curtains a little, the light hurts her eyes?

(SAM partially draws curtain stage left as IRIS supports SILVA [FRED with wig, dark glasses and long silver robe] into room and guides her to downstage chair doing both voices.)

SILVA. Don't expect the life and soul of they party with this copulating head.

IRIS. Sit and listen. Do you know what everyone in this room thought? *(SILVA shakes head.)* They were convinced you and I were the same person.

SILVA. Silly vaginas.

IRIS. Can you imagine such an elaborate charade? And so unperceptive of them, I'm an inch shorter than you, several pounds heavier and a lot older.

SAM. We never doubted that—

IRIS. SHUT UP!! *(Her eyes are fixed on SILVA. Hysteria rises to a climax as IRIS sees only the grotesqueness of her image slumped in the chair.)* As if I would ever want to be you, who would? A barren whore, a foundering singer of songs desperately turning tomorrow into yesterday. A pinnacle of ambition, I'm sure. Silva Ring, facile talents and cheap packaging, an example to envy and emulate? You're an excrescence on my life, you're loathsome. *(She circles SILVA figure. Everyone else frozen.)* What gives you such long life? You were born to cover fear, who needs you? Are you really there? Are you? Are you in there? *(With frenzied searching, clawing gestures she tears off wig, dark glasses and opens the silver robe. FRED is revealed more than a little frightened.)* Where? Where? Whereaaaaaaaaah!

(With a sharp cry she collapses into the floor and into herself, hugged in a tight, rocking ball. They all rush forward to help as the front door rings—long urgent, ceaseless rings.)
(Curtain.)

Scene 3

*(One month later. Morning. SAM staring out of window. He
looks at watch, goes to briefcase and removes a folder of
papers which he lays on the table. Returns to window.
DOLORES enters from kitchen buttoning up a simple black
dress with white collar and cuffs. She crosses to unit.)*

DOLORES. What time is it?
SAM. Five to.

*(DOLORES props an envelope against an award on shelf and
knocks it over.)*

DOLORES. Oh dear. I'm so jumpy.
SAM. No need to be. They say she's fully recovered.
DOLORES. Then why haven't we been allowed to visit
her for the last four weeks?
SAM. They thought it best and she didn't ask.
DOLORES. How could she, poor love? Strapped down,
drugged and electrocuted ... or worse.
SAM. She's been in the London Clinic, not a South American jail.
DOLORES. You're at their mercy if you don't have a relative.
SAM. You could say she took her sister with her.
DOLORES. Don't.

*(She is checking the room obsessively. Sometimes moving an
object an inch then back again.)*

SAM. Dolores. Why are you dressed like that?

DOLORES. What? Why is there something wrong with it?

SAM. No it's ablaze with normality. Should give her quite a shock.

DOLORES. I'd best go and change then.

SAM. Leave it, she'll be here any minute. Besides, the doctors say she's changed too ... a bit.

DOLORES. There's another thing—what do we call her?

SAM. Silva ... I think. Yes, definitely Silva.

(Pause.)

DOLORES. What time is it?

SAM. Time.

DOLORES. It's not right. Someone should've fetched her. She's still a Star.

SAM. She wanted to come out alone. The doctors think it's important.

DOLORES. Can it happen again, Sam?

SAM. It can but Dr. Barnaby doesn't think it will; he's Jane's psychiatrist.

DOLORES. Not the best of recommendations. How is Jane?

SAM. Fine. She's flung herself into Yoga with great verve.

DOLORES. She ought to get herself a lover.

SAM. Shouldn't we all! It's the great gnawing need of the Middle Classes.

DOLORES. Oh, this is worse than waiting for a bus. What time—

(DOLORES looks to lobby at sound of door.)

SILVA. *(V.O.)* Anybody home?

(SILVA enters relaxed and looking good with her natural hair. She carried a small case.)

SILVA. Aaaah! Faithful retainers, how lovely.

SAM. Welcome back to the world.

SILVA. Thanks, it looks good.

DOLORES. We have missed you. Here, let me take that.

(DOLORES takes case. SILVA looks at the room calmly.)

SILVA. How sharp and in focus everything looks.

SAM. There are stacks of fan letters and get well messages.

DOLORES. I put them all in the guest room, you can hardly get in.

SAM. Bo Bergman's posted a card from every state in the Union.

DOLORES. And Nicky's phoned nearly every day.

SAM. Lola sent the roses.

SILVA. Sweet. But they shouldn't feel guilty. None of you should. *(She moves slowly to gaze out of window. SAM and DOLORES exchange glances.)* I haven't seen a single paper. What did you tell the Press?

SAM. Nervous exhaustion.

(SILVA turns and laughs.)

SILVA. Sam, how could you? Everyone knows that means urinated out of your mind or plain raving mad.

SAM. Sorry. Coverage has been very sympathetic. Heigh Ho Silva is number five in the Album Charts and climbing.

SILVA. I'd love some coffee, Dolores.

DOLORES. Yes, of course. I'll see to it.

(DOLORES exits to kitchen. SILVA wanders around the room looking at objects.)

SAM. I've brought the proofs of the profile Bo did of you, it's one of the best ever. He did a wonderful job, finally.

SILVA. I knew he would.

SAM. And when you feel up to it there are some papers for

you to go through. Nothing urgent, especially as I've cut my own throat and drawn up a fantastic new contract between us—fantastic for you that is.

SILVA. There's no need, Sam.

SAM. It's long overdue. I also ran a check on your finances. There had been a bit of sloppy book keeping here and there so you'll find some substantial sums transferred to your personal accounts.

SILVA. I don't wonder that Jane keeps trying to kill herself.

(By the unit SILVA picks up envelope.)

SAM. What exactly do you mean by that?

SILVA. Her psychiatrist, Ned Barnaby. He's wildly attractive.

SAM. Mmm yes. I suppose he is a bit magnetic.

SILVA. A bit! He'd set anybody's compass twirling. *(SILVA opens envelope.)* Hunky too. Plays a lot of rugger.

SAM. Does he?

SILVA. *(Reads letter.)* Now, I am worried, seriously worried. I've obviously got a terminal disease with only hours to live.

SAM. What makes you think that?

SILVA. Dolores Payne has offered to work for me for a year without salary.

SAM. She cares for you dearly.

SILVA. Is that any reason for her to punish herself so viciously? What happened while I was away, did you all become Born Again Christians?

SAM. I think we all realized how much we depend on you.

SILVA. Dependence is weakness, dependence is dangerous. Dr. Barnaby says I depended on my image and in so doing lost my true self.

SAM. Ah!

SILVA. You're not impressed?

SAM. I'm over familiar with the jargon.

SILVA. Ah! *(DOLORES enters with a cup of coffee which she places by SILVA.)* Thanks. Sit down both of you, I have an announcement to make. I want you to be the first to know. I'm giving up my career. No more singing, no more busting a gut, 'The End'.

SAM. You can't be serious?

SILVA. I've had plenty of time to think about it.

DOLORES. You'll miss it dreadfully.

SAM. She's right. You feed off your audiences.

SILVA. Not any more. After twenty odd years at the top, my ego's stuffed like a Strasbourg goose.

SAM. But what will you do? You'll go mad.

SILVA. *(Laughs.)* So what's new? No, I'll live, read, travel, make love. Eventually, I want to buy a place in the country.

SAM. Tell me 'with roses round the door', and I'll vomit.

SILVA. I would like to start a garden and watch it grow.

SAM. Sweet Jesus!

DOLORES. I could never live in the country, it's so noisy. All them animals.

SILVA smiles serenely. SAM gets up.)

SAM. They let you out too soon. I'll drive you back. *(SILVA shakes her head.)* Never sing again, ever?

SILVA. The occasional Royal Command Performance or Hospital Charity Concert perhaps.

(SAM picks up briefcase and kisses SILVA on cheek.)

SAM. Good to have you back looking so well. Give me a ring when the drugs have worn off.

SILVA. Thank you, Sam. I'll ring anyway. You and Jane must visit when I'm settled in the country.

SAM. Sure, sure. Bye.

(SAM exits. DOLORES is sniffling into a hanky. SILVA goes to papers SAM left on desk.)

SILVA. What's up with you, Bossy Boots?

DOLORES. It's the end of an era. Sorry, I haven't cried since Churchill's funeral.

SILVA. Save it, I'm not dead yet.

(SILVA's been scanning the papers in an expert manner.)

DOLORES. I might as well be. Life's going to be pretty dreary from now on.

SILVA. *(Shrieks.)* The mean, unmentionable sodomite. Extra four per cent! What a copulating orifice, I'll have him begging on his bended fornicators before I'm through. What a nerve!

(SILVA throws papers wildly in the air.)

DOLORES. Is it time for your medicine?

SILVA. Dolores, stop edging towards the nearest blunt instrument. I'm perfectly normal.

DOLORES. Oh, yes. Yes, I can see you are. Whatever you say, Madam.

SILVA. We can't have you shrinking with fear, you're small enough as it is. Come. *(She holds out her hands and leads DOLORES to sofa.)* You and me, and my hair are going to have a lovely holiday for about six months.

DOLORES. I shall miss all the glamour and the excitement.

SILVA. Come, come now. Do you think Silva Ring's comeback concert is going to be a modest occasion?

DOLORES. But you said ...

SILVA. One has to retire before one can make a comeback. Sam will take about three months to crack and then he'll have to suffer a little extra.

DOLORES. Will you be well enough?

SILVA. What do you think? Don't be misled by my dramatic collapse in this very room. I admit, I was in a slightly strained condition but I could have pulled back at any time. However, finding myself halfway to a nervous breakdown it suddenly seemed the ideal situation, so I confess I rolled with it. I merely added the other half and what a good move that turned out to be.

DOLORES. Tell me.

SILVA. Sympathy has dulled your wits, my girl. Let me count my blessings ... nice rest in the Clinic ... flattering article in magazine ... Nicky left thinking I was thirty nine ... new contract with Sam, which I will better ... Big chunk of money ... new lover—you'll like Ned Barnaby ... a touching and surprising amount of concern and affection ... oh, the list is endless. Not bad for five minutes frothing about on the floor, is it?

(DOLORES gets up slowly and moves to unit.)

DOLORES. I intend to call my book, Madam Caligula.

SILVA. Sounds good. Order me half a dozen copies.

(DOLORES is searching the unit.)

SILVA. I have saved the best blessing till last.

DOLORES. Oh, yes?

SILVA. Yes, and what a plum it is! Cheap labor for one whole year! *(DOLORES turns and glares.)* Bless you. Heaven will reward you, Dolores.

DOLORES. Begging your pardon, Madam, Dolores isn't well. I'm her sister, Dorothy.

(They BOTH begin to laugh as the Curtain Falls.)

END OF PLAY

PROPERTY PLOT

ACT I
Scene 1
Set
On Shelved Unit (st.rt.)
Books
Lots of C.D.'s
Telephone and answer-
    ing machine
Address book
Photographs
C.D. player and tape
    recorder

On low unit (st. lt.)
Wall mirror
Bottles of drink & min-
    eral water
Drinking glasses
Framed gold discs on wall
Modern prints

Center (upstage)
Small table with drawer
Small chair
Big day diary

Center
Two seating units in L shape
Coffee table
Ashtray
Chrome and leather chair
Beer can
Financial Times newspaper
Remote cont. for C.D.

Envelope with banknotes
    in.
Fred: Passport (sm. Eu. one
    Burgundy color. 3"x5")
Sam: Briefcase, typed papers
    and artwork inside.
Bo: Briefcase, Papers and
    photostat birth cert.
Tea trolley
Nicky: Towel
Sam: Sm. bottle of pills; Pen
Plate of scrambled eggs
Fork

Scene 2
Bo: Tape recorder
Two coffee cups
Bunch of roses w/card
Sev. press photographs
Nicky: Football

Scene 3
Vase of roses
Dishes of olives, chips,
    peanuts
Half filled glass
Bottle of mineral water
Nicky: Beer and half a
    sandwich
Dolores: A handwritten
    note
Iris: Small suitcase

ACT II
Scene 1
File with bills, contracts
   papers, check stubs
Notebook and pen
Pocket calculator
Dolores: Sm. round tray w/
   2 glasses of milk
C.D. case w/Silva's pass-
   port inside
London atlas

Scene 2
Large manila envelope
Nicky: Silva's passport

Hostess trolley
Ice bucket
Bottle of champagne

Scene 3
Vase of roses
Sam: Briefcase with folder of
   assorted typed papers
Dolores: Envelope w/hand-
   written letter inside
Silva: Small case
Cup of coffee

COSTUME PLOT

ACT I, Scene 1
   DOLORES: Fluffy bedroom slippers, Glamorous, multi-colored wrap over plain skirt and blouse. Silver cloth turban
   FRED: Jeans, trainers, white shirt, dark sweater
   SAM. Conservative good suit, blue shirt, tie, black shoes
   SILVA: Trouser suit, silver jewelry, pale silk blouse, tote bag, shoes, raincoat (carried)
   BO: Baggy tweed suit, Glasses
   NICKY: short toweling robe

Scene 2
   DOLORES: Bright lurex top. Plain skirt, old cardigan
   SILVA: Loose, flowing chiffon dress
   NICKY: Track suit, trainers

Scene 3
   SILVA: Silver sheath dress, matching shoes
   LOLA: Cocktail dress, wide brimmed hat, court shoes, purse

SAM: Different tie
NICKY: Polo shirt, trousers, sport jacket
BO: Suit, black turtleneck sweater
SILVA/IRIS: Aplain pleated skirt and jacket. Horn rimmed glasses

ACT II Scene 1
IRIS: Candlewick dressing gown over plain white night-dress. Hornrimmed glasses
As SILVA: Silk negligee

Scene 2
DOLORES: Red dress, silver shoes, big hooped earrings
FRED: Bandages on hand.
SILVA. Cowboy boots, stetson hat, sunglasses, raincoat over IRIS's skirt and blouse
BO: Casual jacket and trousers
NICKY: Baseball jacket, jeans, sweatshirt
LOLA: Big wide brimmed, overlarge track suit
FRED: Long silver dress and wig over jeans and t-shirt

Scene 3
SAM: Different tie
DOLORES: Black or navy dress with white collar and cuffs. Handkerchief
SILVA: Elegant simple dress

GROUND PLAN

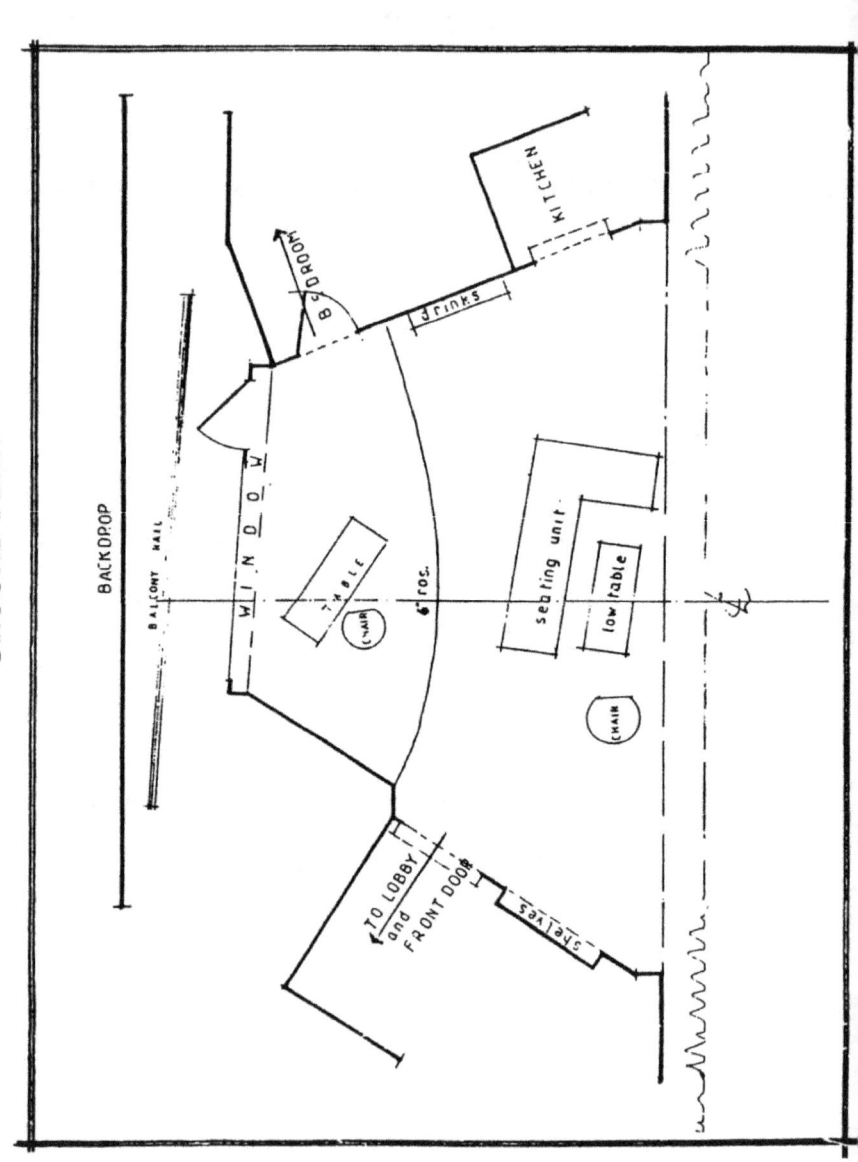

www.ingramcontent.com/pod-product-compliance
Lightning Source LLC
Chambersburg PA
CBHW070351120726
47909CB00008B/2808